EAGLE'S WINGS

GOLDEN FILLY SERIES

EAGLE'S WINGS

LAURAINE SNELLING

BETHANY HOUSE PUBLISHERS
MINNEAPOLIS, MINNESOTA 55438

Published by Bethany House Publishers
A Ministry of Bethany Fellowship, Inc.
6820 Auto Club Road, Minneapolis, Minnesota 55438

Printed in the United States of America

Library of Congress Cataloging-in-Publication Data

Snelling, Lauraine.
    Eagle's wings / Lauraine Snelling.
       p. cm. — (The Golden filly series ; bk. 2)
    Summary: Because her father is ill, without telling her parents, horse-loving Trish earns money after school at the race track, where trouble begins when one of her mounts is in a mysterious accident.

    [1. Horse racing—Fiction. 2. Christian life—Fiction.] I. Title.
II. Series: Snelling, Lauraine. Golden filly series ; bk. 2.
PZ7. S677Eag 1991
[Fic.]—dc20   91–4125
ISBN 1–55661–203–6   CIP
                           AC

To my son Kevin,

who I just realized

is my pattern for David.

Would that every girl

could have a

big brother

like him.

LAURAINE SNELLING is a full-time writer who has authored several published books, sold articles for a wide range of magazines, and written weekly features in local newspapers. She also teaches writing courses and trains people in speaking skills. She and her husband Wayne have two grown children and make their home in California.

Her life-long love of horses began at age five with a pony named Polly and continued with Silver, Kit, Rowdy, and her daughter's horse Cimeron, who starred in her first children's book *Tragedy on the Toutle*.

CHAPTER 1

Tricia Evanston searched the crowd for her mother, a tall woman pushing a wheelchair. Her father had slumped in that chair the moment he sat down again. But he'd been on his feet for the pictures in the winner's circle. Trish and their two-year-old thoroughbred colt, Spitfire, had won their first race. But now her father was gone. Panic welled up.

"Come on, Rhonda." Trish grabbed her life-long friend's arm. "Maybe they're back at the stables."

"Tricia Evanston?" A well-dressed man blocked their way.

"Yes?" She found herself looking up and up.

"I'm Jason Rodgers, owner of Rodgers Stables." He extended his hand. "I've known your father for a long time. It's a real pleasure to meet his daughter."

Trish shook hands with him, wondering where the meeting was going.

"I heard about Hal's illness. It was a relief to see him here today. But let me get right to the point, since I know you have a lot to do. I have an entry in the ninth race tomorrow that I'd like you to ride. Would you be interested?"

Trish nodded before her mouth had time to answer.

7

A mount for Rodgers Stables. The enormity of it walloped the pit of her stomach. "I'd love to but . . . but," she clamped her lips on the brief stammer. After a deep breath, she started again. "That'll be fine." She hoped she sounded grown up—and professional.

But what about Mom and Dad? the thought hit after he'd left. He had already told her when he'd meet her the next day. *I should have asked them first, but then, they never said I couldn't ride for someone else. And I am riding Gatesby for John Anderson. And that crazy horse tries all kinds of shenanigans. But then, I've been training him.*

The thoughts dipped and darted around in her head like bats just out of their cave for the evening.

She looked at Rhonda. The startled look on her face was a mirror of Trish's. Their "all rights!" burst at the same moment.

Both girls turned and loped down the dirt path cutting across the nine-hole golf course in the infield. They met the horses being walked to the saddling paddock for the next race.

"Have you seen Dad?" Trish asked when they reached the stables.

"Your mom took him back to the hospital right after the race," Brad Williams said. Tricia's mother always referred to Trish, her friends Brad and Rhonda, and her brother David as the four musketeers. "He looked pretty bad."

"Where's David?"

"He and Spitfire are still at the testing barn." Brad glanced at his watch. "Should be back any minute."

Trish pulled off her helmet and fluffed her springy

dark bangs with the other hand. "I didn't even get a chance to talk with him."

"Yeah, all that crowd from Prairie kind of took over." Rhonda winked at Trish. "Now you know how the football heroes feel when they get hoisted up on shoulders."

Trish could feel the red heat creeping up her neck again. Doug Ramstead, their high school's star quarterback, had lofted her on his shoulders. All the kids at the track had cheered. It *had* been pretty exciting. Until she saw her father was gone.

At that moment nineteen-year-old David trotted up with Spitfire on the lead line. "You told her?" he asked Brad, then turned to Trish. "Mom said we should come to the hospital as soon as we're done here."

Trish felt like the earth gave out beneath her. "But . . . but you know I can't go in there. I just . . . I . . ." Her gaze darted from Rhonda to David and around the stalls, as if searching for a place to hide. "I can't . . . not to the hospital . . . not now. I'll . . . I'll stay here . . . and . . ." She could feel the tears biting behind her eyelids.

The look David gave her spelled disgust in capital letters. Brad and Rhonda busied themselves on the other side of the cross-tied horse.

Trish leaned her forehead against Spitfire's neck. *Why'd they have to mess up this day? Everything had been perfect so far. Well, not really.* She remembered the empty box in the grandstands. Her father hadn't arrived at the track before the race began. He'd been rushed to the hospital the night before, hardly able to breathe.

It wasn't his first time at the hospital. But she hadn't been able to make herself go to the hospital when he'd been there for several weeks after the cancer was first diagnosed. No matter how hard she'd tried. Or how angry her mother got.

The warm, comforting smell of horse intruded on her thoughts. She stepped back so David could finish rinsing and scraping the water off the animal's blue-black hide. When David unclipped the cross-ties to take Spitfire to the hot walker, Trish took the lead rope. "Let me have him. I'll walk him out."

"You want me to come with you?" Rhonda asked.

Trish shook her head. She swallowed hard and led the weary colt out the stall door.

The noises of the stable receded as they ambled past the last stalls. Trish heard the roar of the stands as another field left the starting gates. She and her dad should be hanging over the fence, studying each horse and rider as they surged around the oval track. He should be pointing out strategies for her as he trained her in the art of becoming a jockey. No one knew racing like her father.

She swiped at a tear that meandered down her cheek. Nothing had been the same since the diagnosis. Her father had lung cancer. And he had talked about the possibility of dying. *And I let him down by not visiting him in the hospital,* Trish scolded herself.

"God, why am I such a chicken?" She aimed her question at the heavens. "Why can't I go see my dad in the hospital?" She kicked a clod of dirt ahead of them.

Spitfire snorted at the interruption. His flicking ears heard all the sounds around them but he was too tired to react. Trish rubbed his nose in a reflex action, her mind on her troubles rather than the horse.

Her mother's accusation, *"You love those horses more than anything,"* joined the battle raging in her mind.

People go to the hospital to die.

Hogwash! People go there to get well.

My dad's not well.

He's better than he was.

Not really. They had to hold him up for the pictures.

Yes, but he made it to the track.

God is supposed to heal him.

Give Him time, you idiot. You want everything right now.

And her mother's voice, *"You love the horses best."*

"No! I don't!" The words burst out of Trish, along with sobs that wrenched her in two.

She leaned into Spitfire's neck and let the tears pour. It wasn't as if she could stop them. All the fear, the anger, the worry, the nagging little doubts that plagued her. All merged with the tears and soaked Spitfire's now dry hide.

The voices died.

Trish hiccupped. She wiped her eyes on her sleeve.

Spitfire bobbed his head, a spear of grass dangling from his teeth. He reached around and nuzzled her shoulder.

When she ignored him, he pushed a bit harder, then blew on her neck.

Trish sniffed again, followed by a deep, shuddery breath.

Spitfire rubbed his muzzle in her hair and licked the remaining salty tear away.

Trish reached up to rub the colt's favorite spot, right behind his ears. He draped his head over her shoulder in contentment.

A new voice seemed to speak in her ear. *If your father could make it to the track for you, weak as he is, we can handle a visit to the hospital for him. No matter what.*

It was as if someone reached over and lifted the killing weights from her shoulders.

Trish nodded. "Come on, Spitfire. I know you're hungry. And Dad is waiting."

She clucked to the colt and the two of them jogged back to the stables.

"If anybody's got any money, we could pick up pizza on the way. I've heard hospital food is terrible." Trish unsnapped the lead line and ducked under Spitfire's neck. Fetlock-deep straw, full water bucket, grain measured, and hay in the manger; all mute evidence that the others had been busy. "Well?" She bit back the slight wobble in her chin as she faced her brother and two best friends. "Let's go."

David threw home the bolt on the stall door. "I have ten dollars, that'll buy one."

"I'm broke but hungry." Trish wrapped her arm around Rhonda's waist.

"Five from me." Rhonda hugged her back.

"I've got eleven dollars," Brad checked his pockets. "And 76 cents. Let's get outta here."

The four piled into the pickup when they reached the parking lot. Brad draped his arm along the back of the seat and whispered in Trish's ear. "I'm proud of you, Tee."

Trish felt a warm spot uncurl and blossom into little stars right down in her middle. She swallowed a couple of leftover tears and rolled her lips together.

Rhonda's hand on her knee telegraphed the same message. They knew she'd fought a private war—and won.

"Hal Evanston's room, please," David said when they stopped at the information desk at the hospital. The aroma of pepperoni and Canadian bacon wafted from the flat cardboard containers Trish and Rhonda carried. Brad had charge of the soft drinks.

The woman at the desk tried to hide a grin as she gave them instructions to room 731.

Shadows hugged the corners of the room where Hal slept in a white-blanketed hospital bed. Marge napped in a chair-bed by his side. Monitors bleeped their rhythm of life, assisted by the slow drip of the IV tube attached to the back of Hal's hand.

Trish wanted to turn and run. Escape down the halls, out the door and back to the barns where life smelled of horse and hay and grain. Where janglings and whinnies and slamming buckets chattered of evening chores and life in the horse lane. That's where her dad should be.

Not here. All was silent and gray. The shadows seemed to have slithered over the rails and painted themselves on his hair and face. His chest barely raised the covers as he breathed in through the oxygen prongs at his nose and out through a dry throat that rasped with the effort.

Trish now knew what an animal felt like in a trap. Why they gnawed off a paw to escape. Only her iron will kept her in the room. *He's going to die. He's going to die.* The words marched through her mind.

"It's not as bad as it looks." Marge rose from her chair to stand by her daughter. "He's just exhausted from going to the track." She put her arm around Trish and hugged her. "You'll never know how glad I am you're here. We have good news. An infection caused this setback and he's responding to the antibiotics."

Trish nodded. She leaned closer to her mother, as if afraid to touch the hand of the stranger sleeping in the bed.

"Maybe we should just go on home and let him sleep," David whispered.

"No." Marge shook her head. "He made me promise to wake him when you got here." She took the drinks from Brad. "You two find some more chairs. We'll have our own celebration right here. Go ahead and wake him, Tee."

"Dad," Trish whispered. When there was no response, she darted a look at her mother.

Marge nodded.

"Dad." This time Trish sounded more like herself. The word wasn't lodged behind the boulder in her throat.

The man in the bed blinked as if his eyelids weighed two pounds each. He frowned in an obvious effort to corral a mind that wandered in exhausted sleep. When he recognized his daughter, a smile crinkled clear to his eyes and sent the shadows skulking back to their corners.

"Congratulations, Tee. You won the race." While faint and scratchy, her father's voice unleashed Trish from a prison of fear. She threw herself into his arms.

"It's okay, Babe," Hal whispered into her ear as one hand stroked her midnight, wavy hair. "I'm going to be all right." His murmur flowed like Trish's when she calmed a frightened horse, soothing and somehow magical. She had learned the music from years of watching and listening to the father she adored.

As her tears subsided, Hal patted her back again. "Hey now, let's get me raised up so we can all talk." He sniffed. "And besides, I smell something good."

Trish wiped her face with a corner of the sheet. She gulped back the remaining tears and sat up on the edge of the bed. "We brought pizza." She heaved a deep breath. "Will they let you . . . I mean . . ."

"No problem," Hal settled himself against the angle of the raised bed. "I'm not in prison, you know."

Trish's grin wobbled but spread. "Coulda fooled me. What'll we use for a table?"

"Improvise." Hal shifted his legs to one side. "We even have a white tablecloth. Hi, Rhonda. Glad you could come." The boys returned with two chairs each and set them around the foot of the bed where Marge had opened the pizza boxes.

Trish scooped out a piece of Canadian bacon with pineapple and handed it on a napkin to her father. Hal bowed his head. "Thank you, Father, for food, for family, for your continued and most needed presence. Amen."

At the unanimous "Amen," they attacked the pizzas. After fingering a stretch of cheese back onto her piece, Trish bit into the gooey concoction as if she hadn't eaten for a week. She licked her lips and took a long drink from her icy Coke.

"How does it feel to win your first race?" Hal asked.

Trish thought a long moment. "Good, great, awesome . . . there just aren't enough words." She shrugged her shoulders. "Spitfire was fantastic. But I almost blew it. I held him back too long."

"Well, you were only doing what I told you. You'll develop a sixth sense about what's best and what your horse can do."

"I hope so." Trish licked her fingers as she finished off her pizza.

"Two men I heard talking were really impressed with Spitfire." David reached for another slice of pizza. "They thought he had a lot more to give."

"And did he?" Hal directed his question to Trish.

She nodded around another mouthful of food. Trish continued to eat as the conversation swirled around her. She could feel the tiredness start at her toes and work its way up her body. She snagged her wandering attention back to the group when she heard her name called.

"I entered Firefly in the seventh race for maiden fillies," Hal said.

Trish nodded.

"Tomorrow."

She jerked upright. "Great. She's ready." *And what*

about your race tomorrow? her inner voice prodded. Trish took a deep swallow from her Coke. "That means I'll have two mounts tomorrow. Mr. Rodgers asked if I'd ride for him in the ninth." She grinned, pleased with the honor. "Good, huh?"

Beeping monitors punctuated the silence.

"But you've never ridden that horse before." Marge rose from her chair. "You don't know anything about it."

"But, Mom, that's what all jockeys do."

"No, not my daughter. I only agreed to your riding our horses."

"You should have talked with us before you accepted the mount." Hal leaned against his pillows, lines deepening around his mouth.

"I know, but there wasn't any time." Trish shoved her fingers through her hair. "And besides, you weren't there to ask." She paused and chewed her lip. "I thought you'd be proud of me."

"Oh, Tee, I am." Hal reached for her hand. "It's just that . . . well, things aren't normal and . . ."

"You call Mr. Rodgers and tell him no, thank you." Marge interrupted.

"Dad!" Trish leaped from her chair.

"We'll talk about it." Hal coughed on a deep breath.

"We better get home and get the chores done." David folded the cover on the empty pizza box. "Come on, Brad, let's put these chairs back."

Trish glanced at her mother. Marge stood looking out the window, her back to the room. Her hand rubbed her elbow as if to warm it. *Or to keep from slamming something or someone,* Trish thought. She knew how much her mother hated the thought of Trish racing. This was just the latest in a long line of discussions.

Then her inner nagger leapt into the battle, *You just went ahead and accepted, before thinking it through.*

Trish had to admit this was true. She'd been so excited at being asked that she hadn't really considered what her mother would say. Until now.

Trish leaned over the bed to kiss her father goodnight. Before he hugged her he slipped a 3 × 5 card into her hand. "Hang on to this," he whispered.

Trish hugged him. "See you tomorrow."

As the others said their goodbyes, Trish looked over at her mom.

"We'll talk more when I get home." Marge clipped her words.

Trish wasn't sure if that was a threat or a promise. She left the room, pausing briefly to read the words on the card before she strode down the hall. "Always and for everything giving thanks in the name of our Lord Jesus Christ to God the Father" (Ephesians 5:20).

Right, she thought, as she stuffed the card in her pocket. *Thank you, God, that my mother is ready to kill me . . . again?*

CHAPTER 2

I'm in for it again, Trish thought.

Dusk softened the outlines of trees and fences as the pick-up turned into the drive of Runnin' On Farm. Falling dew raised ground mist that puddled in the pasture hollows and lapped up the ridges. Caesar barked a welcome, frisking beside the truck as David braked to a stop.

Trish pulled her frame upright and slid from the cab. "I'll change and be right down." She turned toward the house. "Come on, Rhonda." Trish bent over to give Caesar his expected strokes, scratching behind his pointed Collie ears and fluffing his white ruff. A flash nose-lick thanked her.

"You think you'll get it bad?" Rhonda asked as they sprinted up the three back steps.

"I could tell Mom's really mad but Dad knows how important riding is to me. To the farm. We need the money now that Dad's so sick." She pulled off both high boots at the boot jack by the sliding glass door. "I just hate having her mad at me. You know how much I hate fighting . . . of any kind."

"Yeah," Rhonda nodded soberly. "Me, too."

The usual disaster area greeted them as they entered Tee's bedroom. She ignored the unmade bed and dug a pair of jeans out of the pile of clothes tossed on the chair. A minute's rummaging located a sweatshirt at the bottom of another pile.

Rhonda stared at the mess. "Maybe you should just stay up here and clean your room." She shook her head. "That would make her happier than anything."

"Later." Trish inspected the spots on her white racing pants. "Gotta remember to throw these in the washing machine. I'll need them tomorrow."

Thoughts of her mother and the coming argument flitted away on the evening breeze as Trish trotted down to the stables. A deep breath told her someone was burning leaves. Caesar leaped in front of them and whined for attention. Both girls stopped to stroke the dog's sable coat.

The stables seemed empty with the racing string at the track. "Miss Tee and her mother need some exercise." Trish measured grain into a bucket for the mare and handed Rhonda a hunk of hay. As they left the feedroom, she stuck a curry comb in her back pocket and dropped a soft brush on top of the grain.

A nicker greeted them when they entered the shadowed barn. Trish flicked on the lightswitch and the bay mare blinked at the glare. She nickered again at the sight of the grain and hay.

"Hungry, are you?" Trish held out a handful of grain. "You need to get out first, then eat." The mare lipped the grain, then nudged Trish's chest, begging for more. Trish took the lead rope down from its hook and clipped it to the mare's halter. "Hi, Miss Tee, whatcha hiding for?"

Rhonda giggled at the month-old filly who peeked out from behind her bay mother, whose long black tail hairs whisked over Miss Tee's face. "You should know me by now." Rhonda's soft voice set the foal's ears flicking.

Trish offered the lead shank to Rhonda and opened the stall. She smoothed the mare's shoulder as she slipped inside. "Come on, Baby. You don't need to play hide-and-seek with me."

The foal stretched her nose as far as she could, then took two steps. When Trish touched the soft muzzle, Miss Tee leaped back. She shook her head and stamped one tiny forefoot.

"Okay for you," Trish turned her back. "Hand me that brush, will you?" When Rhonda handed her the brush, Trish stroked it down the mare's neck. She winked at Rhonda and whistled a little tune, all the while ignoring the foal.

Step by step Miss Tee left her hideout and approached her owner. Finally she rubbed her forehead on Trish's arm.

"Silly baby," Trish crooned as she gently rubbed the filly's ears. "Just have to play out your games, don't you?"

"What a clown." Rhonda laughed as she swung the stall open. "Does she always act like that?"

"No, only when I haven't paid enough attention to her. The last couple of days have been kind of crazy."

"You're telling me." Rhonda rolled her eyes.

"Why don't you walk them and I'll muck out this stall."

"What a deal." Rhonda took the lead rope. She

clucked to the mare and the three trotted out of the barn. Miss Tee stopped at the door and looked back at Trish as if asking why she wasn't coming too.

"Go on, run a bit. You don't have all night." Trish shooed the filly out and reached for the pitchfork.

It was eight o'clock by the time the four of them finished all the chores and Brad drove his blue Mustang out the drive.

"I'm beat." Trish shrugged her shoulders up to her ears to pull out the kinks.

"Me too." David scratched Caesar's head. "I'm going to bed."

I wish, Trish thought. "You could do my chemistry problems."

"In your dreams, girl." David threw her a big-brother's-pained-with-his-sister look. "That's not how you learn the stuff."

"Thanks. I don't seem to be learning it too well anyway."

"Tell you what, I'll help you tomorrow night. If you have any questions, hold 'em."

Trish nodded. She took another deep breath on the way to her room and rotated both shoulders again. Her feet felt like they each weighed a ton. As did her eyelids. She groaned at the state of her room. With one hand she scooped up her racing silks, both top and pants, then grabbed some other good pants and shirts to add to the wash load. She didn't dare ask her mother to wash clothes, or even come into the room. It was bad enough arguing about racing, not to mention their on-going fight over Trish's housekeeping habits. Or lack of them, as the room attested.

After starting the machine, Trish bit her bottom lip. This once wouldn't hurt. And besides, studying was more important than a clean room. Wasn't it?

She opened her closet door and tossed in the pile of clothes off the chair. The two stacks on the floor were quickly shoved under the bed. Maybe a Diet Coke would help her stay awake. Back down the hall. And an apple.

"I thought you had to study," David growled from the couch where he was stretched out watching TV.

"I am. I mean, I do." Trish stuck her head in the open refrigerator. "Did you drink all the Diet Coke?" Not waiting for an answer, she located the last one, behind the milk. She polished the apple on the front of her sweatshirt and bit into the shiny red skin. "Thought you were going to bed," she commented around chewing the apple.

"Don't talk with your mouth full."

"Yes, Mother." Trish ducked the pillow he threw at her and headed back to her room. At least it *looked* better. She set her Coke down on the desk and pulled out the chair. Papers slid to the floor. With a groan she picked up the pieces of her term paper. *That* was ready for a rewrite. The card from her father caught her eye as she plunked down on the chair. The hard, uncomfortable, stiff chair. She looked longingly at the bed.

Hard to do, she thought, as she tacked the card up above the desk. "Give thanks in everything." Sure. Even chemistry?

With a yawn she opened the book.

You've been stalling, her little voice scolded.

"I'm just tired," she caught herself answering aloud. "So shut up."

The first problem made sense. Now that was some kind of breakthrough. Trish sipped her Coke, mentally rehearsing the list of chemical symbols. The next problem took a little longer. The fourth problem . . .

"Trish, wake up." Marge shook her for the second time.

"Huh—h-h." Trish blinked her eyes open. She stretched her neck where it crinked from lying on her crossed arms, on top of her chemistry book. "Hi, Mom."

"Get to bed," Marge patted her daughter's shoulder. "You aren't getting anywhere this way."

"What time is it?"

"Ten."

Trish blinked again. Everything seemed furry around the edges. "I need to finish this assignment."

"Bed." Marge closed the book.

———

Trish wanted nothing more than to shut off the alarm in what seemed like only minutes after she'd pulled the covers up.

"You'd better hustle." David knocked on her door.

Trish slept on the way to the track. Even the chill of a drizzly morning failed to wake her. She had reached the truck with her eyes half-closed and promptly fallen back asleep.

"Well, Sleeping Beauty, you better wake up now or Gatesby'll do it for you." David pushed her toward the door.

The thought brought her alert—immediately. You didn't sleep or even blink around Gatesby. The least you'd get would be a nip on whatever part of your anatomy the crazy horse took a shine to, the worst . . . well, so far the worst had taken a week to heal. At least neither one of them had broken anything in that fall on the home track.

Spitfire slammed a hoof against his stall door. His whicker was not a plea but a demand.

"I'll saddle Firefly while you get him ready," David nodded at Spitfire. "Then you can ride Gatesby and I'll take Final Command. We should be done in an hour that way. Dad said to keep it slow and easy this morning. Just loosen them up. They deserve a day of rest, too."

Some day of rest, Trish thought as she brushed and saddled the restless black. *We're rushing like crazy and I have two races this afternoon.* She felt her butterflies stretching their wings . . . right in her middle.

"You were fantastic, fella," she rubbed Spitfire's ears before leading him out of the stall. "Ready, David."

The workout ran smoothly except for one brief shy at a blowing paper. While the drizzle had stopped, gray clouds and a bone-penetrating wind made Trish think of hot chocolate and warm blankets. At least she'd remembered her gloves. Spitfire showed only slight traces of sweat when she returned to the stables. Trish pulled the saddle off and clipped him to the hot walker.

Gatesby appeared in a good mood. The bright sorrel nickered when he saw her and even kept his ears forward when she stepped into the stall. Trish clipped the cross-ties to his halter and turned around for the saddle she'd left on the stall door.

"Ow-w-w! You ornery idiot! And here I thought you were happy to see me." She rubbed her left shoulder. It stung even through the windbreaker, down vest and sweatshirt.

Gatesby flung his head as far up as the shanks allowed and rolled his eyes.

"He's laughing at you." David handed her the bridle.

"Yeah, I'm sure he thought it was a love bite," Trish grumbled as she finished tacking him up.

"Naw, he just loves to bite." David had his cupped hands ready as she led the dancing horse out of the stall. "Now you be careful with him."

"David," Trish put both hands on her hips. "You're beginning to sound just like Mom. Worry, worry, worry. You know I watch this guy like a . . ."

"Right. And how's your shoulder?"

Gatesby perked his ears toward the track as Trish loosened the reins. While he never succeeded in a flat-footed walk, at least he skipped any crow-hopping or sudden lunges. Trish reined him down tight any time another horse galloped by. Gatesby wanted to race, not slow gallop.

Trish made the mistake of wiping her drippy nose on her sleeve and had to manhandle the bit out of his teeth before he made more than ten strides. "Sneaky aren't you? Well sorry, boy, but the boss said an easy lope. You're working up a lather just fighting me. Now settle down."

Gatesby snorted and tossed his head but quit fighting. When they returned to the stables, he blew in her face, as if in gratitude for a good ride. Quickly they clipped Gatesby and Final Command on the hot walker, forked the manure piles out to the wheelbarrow and filled water buckets. Trish measured grain and tossed hay wedges in the mangers as David returned the animals to their stalls.

"See you guys later," Trish blew Spitfire a kiss as she climbed back in the truck. She glanced at her watch. "You better gun it, Davey boy. We used up our breakfast time and showers are out."

The creases on Marge's forehead warned them to hurry when they reached home. One glance at her watch took the place of a thousand words.

"I know. We're hurrying." Trish shucked her jacket and boots. *One thing I know,* she thought as she changed clothes with the speed of a frantic shopper, *I never have time to worry.*

The car seemed empty without her father. And she hadn't even called him last night. But then she hadn't done a lot of things last night. She finished the peanut butter toast her mother had handed her on the way out the door and wiped her mouth with the napkin. *I'd think that with all the stuff going on, we could miss church one Sunday. Surely*—She shut the rebellious thoughts down. Today her attitude had better be perfect. She got out of the discussion last night, but knowing her mother, the war wasn't over yet. If *only* she wasn't such a worrier. And liked racing better. Like Hal and Trish did. Then life would be so simple.

Trish greeted her friends as they entered the church. One of these days she'd like to go back to youth group too. There just wasn't enough time for everything. She grinned at Rhonda when Marge led them into the pew just behind the Seabolt family.

"Can you come to the track?" Trish whispered as they sat down.

Rhonda shook her head. "My grandmother's coming for dinner."

Marge's frown canceled their conversation.

Trish's eyes drooped during the scripture reading. She perked up when the folk group sang a new song. The chorus played in her mind long after the song was finished. "And He will raise you up on eagle's wings . . ."

Trish felt herself jerk. She'd gone to sleep. Her mother's warning "Trish" came just as David drilled her with his elbow. Trish blinked and squinted. She'd slept right through the sermon.

One more thing to add to her mother's list.

CHAPTER 3

Trish breathed a sigh of relief.

"We'll see you at the track." Marge paused just before going out the door. "Trish, be careful. You know I . . ." She shook her head, her forehead furrowing again. "David, just make sure she's safe."

"Don't worry, Mom. You take care of Dad." David gently pushed her out the door. "We'll be fine."

Marge nodded, obviously not convinced. She dropped a quick kiss on both David's and Trish's cheeks and left.

Trish's deep breath seemed to give her butterflies a boost instead of calming them. *Saved again*, she thought. *Maybe if we keep postponing, she'll forget to holler at me.* No, if there was one thing her mother did well, it was worry about Trish's racing.

She chewed on her lip. "Oh, no! My silks. They're not dry."

"Well, you better get a move on." David shouted from his room where he'd gone to change clothes.

"Yes, Mother." Trish stuck out her tongue. He sounded too much like Mom for comfort. The list of all she needed to take ran through her mind as she hurried to the laundry room. Her silks, shirts and

29

pants all hung on hangers on the bar above the dryer, ready to take. "Thanks, Mom," Trish breathed as she grabbed the hangers. A twinge of guilt at the mess on the floor attacked her when she hung the clothes in her closet. *Soon*, she promised herself. *Soon I'll get all this cleaned up again.*

Her mother's advice, more like nagging in Trish's opinion, ran through her mind. *Just hang your things up when you take them off, or put them in the hamper and your room will stay neat.*

"You ready?" David knocked on his sister's door. "I'm going down to the barn to check on things, so you have five minutes. Oh, and remember to call Dad."

Trish packed the last of her gear in her sports bag and slipped the garment cover over her silks. Her glance fell on the cards tacked to her wall. The verses, written in her father's square printing, reminded her to pray. "Please, make my Dad well." She picked up her bag. "And take care of us today. Thanks for everything." She turned off her light. "Oh, and help me win. Amen."

She didn't recognize the voice that answered the phone in her father's hospital room. Though weak and scratchy, it had to be Hal. No one else shared his room. "Dad?"

"Good morning, Tee." He cleared his throat.

"You sound awful."

"I know. I just haven't talked much yet." He coughed once, gingerly, as if his chest hurt.

"Mom's on her way there. David and I are leaving in a couple of minutes."

"Good. We've drawn the post for Firefly so you

need to get her out in front and let her go. How was the track?"

"Dry. It didn't rain, just mist, and it looks like it may clear off."

"That's great. And Tee, take some time and go over to see Rodger's mount. Get to know him a little. Jason'll tell you how he wants the race run so you can concentrate on the horse. You've a gift there, so use it."

"Thanks, Dad." Trish heard the truck horn honking. "Gotta go. See you at the track."

Trish focused on relaxing during the drive to Portland Meadows. She took deep breaths and held them before exhaling. The butterflies delighted in the extra oxygen. She scrunched her shoulders up to her ears. Her fluttering friends did aerial flips.

Trish shook her head. Might as well watch the sailboats on the Columbia River for all the good her efforts did.

"Uptight?" David asked as they crossed the I–5 bridge between Vancouver and Portland.

"Yep. This is the first time I'm racing a horse I haven't ridden before."

"I know. And only your third race."

"Thanks for reminding me."

"You want a hamburger before we get there?" David pointed at the golden arches off to the right.

Trish gave him her best my-but-you're-dumb-big-brother look.

"Okay. Okay. I'll just get one for me." David pulled off the freeway.

"I'll take a Diet Coke," Trish added to his order.

Sipping the drink seemed to help. *Maybe butterflies like Diet Coke*, Trish thought.

David flashed their passes as they entered the stable area to the east of the track. "Trish," he said, slowing for a blanketed horse being led across the drive, "you *will* be careful."

"About what?"

"When you're racing, dopey."

"Now you sound like Mom. You want to be a worrier too?"

"Well, just don't take any unnecessary chances."

Trish snorted. "What do you think I am, dumb?"

"No, you just want to win . . . a lot."

Brad had three of their horses working the hot walker while he cleaned their stalls. Only Gatesby and Spitfire pleaded for release when Trish hung her gear in the tack room. Ol Dan'l whickered a greeting from his place on the exerciser.

"Boy, you've been hard at it." Trish greeted her friend. "How come you left those two inside?"

"Right. And thanks to you, too." Brad leaned on his pitchfork. "I didn't want to break his record. Why, Gatesby hasn't had a bite out of anyone for nearly 24 hours."

Trish chuckled as she entered Spitfire's stall. The black colt nuzzled her shoulder and dropped his head against her chest to have his ears rubbed. Trish obliged, enjoying the ritual as much as her horse. She'd cared for him since he was foaled, trained him, and finally they'd raced. She was the only rider he'd ever had. With her he behaved, most of the time. He wasn't named Spitfire for nothing.

Trish stroked his coarse black forelock and smiled at his sleepy-eyed contentment. "What a baby you are," she murmured as she snapped a lead shank to his halter. "How about some time outside?"

The horse perked up. His ears pricked forward and he snorted in her ear as she led him outside. She clipped him to the hot walker and laughed as he half-reared and shook his head. David finished laying the straw bedding as she led Dan'l back into his stall.

"Come on, I'll help you with Gatesby, then you get over to meet Rodger's horse while we groom these guys."

Trish gave Dan'l a last pat. Guilt over her neglect of her old friend nibbled at her mind. There just wasn't enough time for all she *had* to do, let alone the things she *wanted* to do.

"Now, you behave!" She snapped the rope on Gatesby's halter. David copied her motions so they had him cross-tied between them. Gatesby walked out of the stall and over to the hot walker without even a snort. He joined the other horses in their circular path, plodding like an old plowhorse.

"Is he sick?" Trish flashed back to the infection that had raged through their stables a month ago.

"Nah-h-h." David shook his head. "Just disappointed cause we were ready for him."

"Okay. Well, I'll be back in a while."

The Rodgers Ranch sign creaked a greeting in a puff of breeze. All the stalls and walkways showed the detail to attention of a first-rate stable. *Why would he ask you to ride?* her inner voice whispered in her ear.

Any jockey's anxious to ride for him. Trish shrugged.

As her dad always said, never look a gift horse in the mouth. Or in this case, a gift ride.

"Your mount's down here," the trainer said after asking Trish about her father. "We've always thought this old boy had more to give, but somehow he's never come in higher than fourth. He's a good horse, gentle as can be, and from a good line. His registered name is Prancer's Dandy but we call him Dandy."

Just needs a fire under him, Trish thought as she dug in her pocket for the chunk of carrot she always kept there. The dark bay lipped it off her palm and munched the treat. Trish stood still in front of him, waiting for the horse to finish his inspection of her. When he'd sniffed her hand, up her arm and then her hair, he tossed his head as if giving a nod of approval. Trish grasped his blue web halter with one hand and rubbed up behind his ear with the other.

"So we're gonna race today, Dandy boy." She knew it wasn't what she said but the tone of her voice that set the dark ears twitching. She kept up her sing-song rhythm as she stroked the wide white blaze between his eyes and down over his muzzle. "You're a sweetheart. You know that, don't you?" Dandy nodded, leaning into her magic fingers.

"I see you've made a friend." Jason Rodgers joined them.

"Good morning, Mr. Rodgers." At his greeting Trish felt one or two of her butterfly troupe somersault. "He sure is a friendly horse."

"True, but we need some fire from him. I may enter Dandy in a claiming race if he doesn't do something soon. Make sure you have a whip with you today. I want you to do all you can to make him want to run his best."

Trish took a deep breath. "Yes, sir. Well, Dandy," she scratched him under the throat one more time, "see you in the saddling paddock."

Trish missed having Rhonda along as she headed for the dressing room under the grandstand. She, David and Brad had spent the last hours grooming their horses. Firefly fairly gleamed from all the brushing. While she wasn't the blue-black of Spitfire, her four white socks sparkled against the dark color of her legs. A small diamond between her eyes left white hairs whenever the filly rubbed against Trish's shoulder. Today Firefly was ready to run. It was as if she knew her turn was coming, the way the filly looked to the grandstands every time the roar of the crowd announced another start.

The women's locker room was a total disaster as Trish entered the door. Towels, bags, boots and tired women draped everywhere. Liniment and lather from earlier races vied for supreme billing on the moisture-heavy air.

"Hi, Trish." Genie Stokes, the jockey who exercised for Runnin' On Farm in the mornings, waved from a bench in the corner. "There's room for you over here." She pushed a bag and jacket out of the way.

"Thanks." Trish hung her silks on the hook above the green bench. "Congratulations on that win today. You riding again?"

"Yeah. Against you in both the seventh and the ninth."

"Oh."

"Don't worry. You'll do fine. Firefly is posted as a favorite." Genie stretched her arms over her head and twisted from side to side. "How's your dad?"

Trish felt the heavy weight settle back on her shoulders. She'd been hoping her father would make it to the stables before she left to dress. But he hadn't. And their box in the grandstand was still empty too. "He says he's feeling better again. They plan on being here today."

"Your dad's a good man. You're lucky he's trained you, you know."

"Yeah. Thanks." Trish slipped to the floor to begin her warm-up routine. Ham-string stretches, curl-ups, push-ups, her body followed the patterns, and the rhythms bottled up the fears trying to crowd her mind.

Once she was dressed and weighed in, lead weights inserted in the saddle pad slots, she flexed her arms. The silky fabric felt cold against her heated skin. "Thank you, Father," she prayed as she ambled down the tunnel to the saddling paddock, "for the chance to race again. Help me do my best. And please make my dad better." Her soft voice disappeared in the noise from the stands. Horse racing was not a quiet sport.

David and Firefly occupied the first stall since they'd drawn the post position. He buckled the saddle girth and cupped his hands to boost Trish up. "You can do it." He patted her white-clad knee. "Brad's waiting for you."

Trish took a deep breath and let it out slowly. She gathered her reins and leaned forward to rub Firefly's shiny neck. "Okay, girl. This is it. Let's use those eagle's wings." The melody of the song trickled through her mind like a calming stream on a summer's day.

Firefly liked the crowd. She pranced beside Dan'l like a queen bowing to her subjects. Ears nearly touching, chin tucked to her chest, she danced down the track. At the turn, when Brad loosened the lead shank, Firefly broke into a canter, her body collected, every muscle and sinew primed for the breaking strides.

She entered the gate, again behaving like the lady she was. Firefly even remained flat-footed when the horse next to her reared and nearly unseated the jockey.

The hush fell, that moment when all the world seems to wait on tiptoe for the shot.

Trish crouched forward. The gun, the gate and Firefly's burst for freedom seemed to explode at the same moment. Her "GO!" disappeared in the thunder of the race.

Firefly took the post like a veteran. Each stride lengthened, hurtling her forward. Trish concentrated on her horse, at the same time staying aware of the horses on her right.

Firefly tugged at the bit. Her ears swept back and forth listening to Trish's encouraging song. The horse flattened out, reaching for the finish as each furlong post flashed by. As they crossed the wire, Firefly was still begging for more slack. No other horse even came close. They won by a furlong.

The stands went wild. Trish heard the roar now that she could relax. "Wow! Oh, Baby, you're awesome." She patted the steaming neck, then settled back in the saddle so she could snap her goggles up on her helmet. "You not only won, you ran away from the pack." Firefly jogged sideways on her approach to the winner's circle, her neck curved, head high, as befits a reigning monarch.

She posed for the pictures, as if nodding to the flash. Trish and David grinned at each other. But their father's place in the picture as owner was empty.

"Mom called," David said as they led Firefly away. "Dad's okay but they decided since yesterday wore him out so bad, they'd skip today. They're waiting for you to call when you're done. He said good luck on your next race, too."

Trish hugged Firefly one more time before David led the filly off to the testing barn. "If only Dad could have seen this," she whispered to her steaming mount. "He'd be so proud of you. And here we thought Spitfire was our big winner."

Trish felt strange in blue and green silks. Even her butterflies didn't like the new colors. She felt like a royal battle waged in her middle. The whip in her hand didn't help either. But Mr. Rodgers had insisted that she carry—and use it.

The saddling paddock, round—with stalls radiating out like spokes on a wheel—felt different without David and Brad there to cheer her on. She gathered her reins after the boost into the saddle. Dandy pricked his ears at her voice. She leaned forward to stroke his neck and smooth his black mane to one side.

"Ready?" At Trish's nod, the trainer untied the slipknotted rope and backed Dandy out of his stall. They joined the parade to the post, in the middle of the pack, position number three.

"Lord, we really need those eagle's wings this time," Trish included the prayer in her monologue. "Sure hope you have more than one pair. Firefly flew on hers." They broke into a canter at the turn. Dandy seemed alert and raring to go. *But he doesn't have the class of our horses*, Trish thought as she guided him into the gate. *Guess I'm already spoiled.*

Her whip hit his haunches as the gate swung open. Dandy bolted forward, his ears laid back. "Sorry, fella, but that's the way it goes." Trish leaned forward, her goggles brushing his mane. "Come on now!" Dandy settled into an ever-lengthening stride. As they rounded the first turn, Trish encouraged him again, this time taking him to the rail, just behind the front runner. When a horse came up on their right, Dandy lengthened his stride again. And kept his position.

The far turn found the field bunched behind them. When Dandy slowed a bit, Trish tapped him with the whip again, her voice commanding in his ears, "Come on, Dandy, give it all you've got." He laid his ears back again and drove down on the front runner.

They finished second, by half a body length.

"Wow-ee!" Trish felt like throwing her whip in the air and screaming for joy. They hadn't won, but Dandy'd been tagged as last in the field. What a long shot.

"Incredible." Jason Rodgers shook her hand. "He's never run like that. How about riding for me Wednesday? If you can get Dandy to run like that, I'd like you on my other horses, too." He handed her an envelope.

"Thank you, and I'd love to." Trish shook his offered hand. "What race?"

"How about the third and the seventh?"

Trish stopped in her tracks. The third? School wouldn't be out yet. "Sorry," she shook her head. "I could do the seventh but I'm not out of school till after three."

"That's fine. I'll see you then."

But what's your mother going to say when she hears this? her inner-nagger gloated.

CHAPTER 4

"You're awfully quiet." David steered the truck into the hospital parking lot.

Trish's sigh originated somewhere down about her toes. She'd agreed to ride for Rodgers before she had asked her parents. And her mom was upset over today's ride. What would she say about riding Wednesday? *But I won't be missing any school. At least I thought of that.* She tried to make things all right in her mind before she needed to explain to anyone else but it wasn't easy. In fact, she knew she was in the wrong. Again.

"It's nothing, really," she answered David with a shrug. "Just tired, I guess."

The hospital corridors seemed to close in on her as she and David left the elevator. While she tried to walk quietly, her booted heels tapped out echoes to match those marching in her mind. *You better get a smile on,* she ordered herself. *You're a winner, remember?*

"Hi, Dad, Mom." Trish leaned over the bed to give her dad a hug. "You look better than yesterday."

"Sorry we didn't make it to the track." Hal pressed the button to raise his head, then shifted to a comfortable position against the pillows.

41

"The doctor gave him a choice of going home a day earlier or going to the track today," Marge explained.

"And I *need* to get out of here." Hal patted the bed beside him. "Congratulations, Tee. Sounds like you and Firefly ran some race."

"She was having fun out there." Trish gave a little bounce. "You should have seen her. That horse loves the crowd—you'd think all the applause was for her. And now that she knows how much attention she gets for winning . . . well, just try to keep her back."

"And we'd counted so hard on Spitfire. Now we have two winners. That's wonderful!" Hal took a sip of water to soothe his throat. "How'd you do with the Rodgers' horse?"

"A second. Mr. Rodgers could hardly believe it. And he gave me this, besides what I'll get as part of the purse." She handed her father the envelope. "Every little bit will help with the entry fees."

"No, Trish. That's your money. You earned it, you bank it."

"But, Dad."

"No, I mean it. We've never expected you kids to help with the bills and we won't start now."

But this is different, Trish thought. *You've never been sick before and you've always had so many horses to train, you've turned some away. Now we only have Anderson's two.* She glanced over at her mother but seeing the frown on her face, wisely left it at that.

After some casual banter about other things, Marge finally asked, "Have you kids eaten yet?"

"No, but we'll fix something at home." David rose from his chair. "We've got the chores to do."

"Where's Brad?"

"He had to do something with his mom and dad tonight, so we're it."

"How much homework do you have?" Marge turned to Trish.

"Not much." Trish rolled her lips together. She wasn't lying, exactly. It all depended on how you defined much.

"Well, David, you do the chores so Trish can study."

"Why doesn't *he* do my chemistry and I'll feed the mares." Trish knew she'd made a mistake the minute the careless words were out of her mouth. "Just a joke." She backtracked as fast as she could. "Come on, Mom. Just a joke."

"When will you learn?" David asked as they walked back down the hall after their goodbyes.

Trish just shook her head. And *he* didn't know the half of it.

Trish fixed tuna fish sandwiches when they got home. She took hers into her bedroom and after changing clothes, sat down at her desk. The glow from the desk lamp pooled on her chemistry book and the paper with only two problems done. She'd better hit it hard.

Two hours later she rose and stretched. Chemistry caught up. Spanish reviewed. Only one composition to go—and that only two pages. But her eyes felt like someone had thrown a handful of sand in them.

She thought longingly of a hot bath as she stumbled to the kitchen for something to drink. David sprawled on the sofa, dead to the world, while the TV flickered in the corner.

"Hey, why don't you sleep in bed." Trish prodded his shoulder.

"Um-m-m." David didn't even open his eyes. "Just waiting for Mom."

Car lights flashed in the window as Trish poured herself a glass of milk. She felt like sprinting down the hall and hiding in her room.

Marge hung her coat in the closet. "Hi, kids. Any messages?"

"Forgot to check." Trish looked at the answering machine. "It's flashing. I gotta finish a paper." She left her mother to deal with the machine and headed back to her books.

Another hour, and she slipped her recopied paper into her notebook. What a way to end a winning day; all her homework caught up. Except reviewing history—but the test wasn't until Tuesday, she reasoned. No more studying tonight. Her bed was calling.

" 'Night, Mom." Trish took her plate and glass back to the kitchen. Marge was still on the phone.

Trish slung her jeans and sweatshirt over the chair. She planned on putting them on again in the morning, so why hang them up? She'd just turned out the light when Marge tapped at the door.

"Trish?"

"Yeah, I'm awake." *Here it comes,* Trish thought. *And what do I do about Wednesday?*

Marge turned the lamp back on. She started to sit down in the desk chair but frowned at the clothes draped across the back. Instead she sat at the foot of Trish's bed.

"Your father and I've been talking . . ."

I'll just bet, Trish thought as she folded her arms behind her head.

"You *know* how much I hate your racing at the track."

"Yeah."

"But I agreed to go along with what your father said. You could race *our* horses."

"But, Mom . . ."

"No, let me finish." Marge paused, as if searching for the right words. "Trish, I don't want you racing for other stables. You don't know those horses and you haven't had a lot of experience yet."

"But that's how I'd get more experience." Trish couldn't keep her mouth closed.

"You're only sixteen. You don't need more experience racing; you need time for school. Your studies have to come first."

"But, Mom." Trish sat up and hugged her knees. "Racing is all I want to do and I'm doing okay in school, too."

"Okay isn't good enough. You are too bright to waste your brain riding horses. You can pull straight A's when you work at it."

All Trish heard was "waste." "What do you mean *waste*? You think Dad wastes his time training horses? That's our business, Mom, and his dream. We've always talked about when I could jockey for our horses. And now all *you* want is for me to go to school. Other kids go out for sports—mine is just a different one." Trish could hear her voice getting louder. She knew she should calm down, but she couldn't. "And besides, I made good money today."

"Trish, let me finish."

"Why bother? All you do is try to take away the thing I love most." Trish turned her head, struggling to keep the tears back.

"Listen to me, I was trying to explain . . ." her mother went on. "I didn't want you racing at all, but I went along with *our* horses. Your father said you can race for other farms but you have to talk it over with him. That's not my idea, but he *is* your father." The deep furrows creased her forehead. She spit the words out as if she were holding something back. "No matter how hard I try to talk sensibly with you, you get upset."

"I didn't start this." Trish thumped back on her pillow. "Racing is *not* a waste!"

"That's enough!"

"No! If I got a job at the Burger Palace, you'd think that was okay. But I made more money in one race . . . than . . . than." Trish couldn't think far enough. "And you call it a waste. We *need* the money. You know that."

"That's enough. If you can't talk to me without yelling . . ."

Look who's talking, Trish corralled her thoughts. *Just leave me alone.* She glared at her mother through tear-filled eyes.

Marge stood to leave. "Genie Stokes will be working all the horses at the track in the morning. David will do the chores both here and at The Meadows. And you will go to school . . . *on time for a change.*" The click of the closing door sounded like a gunshot in the stillness.

Great. Trish rolled on her side and pulled the covers

up. *I'm the only one who's ever ridden Spitfire. Let 'em find out the hard way.* I am *going to ride.*

But what about Wednesday? her little voice asked.

She shrugged off the thought and drifted to sleep. When she awoke in the morning Trish realized her dreams hadn't been pleasant ones. She felt like she'd been in a battle all night. What *would* she do about Wednesday? How would she get to the track? She'd given her word to Mr. Rodgers. She wouldn't be missing any school. *But* she didn't have her parents' permission. What would they do when they found out? They really needed the money; she knew the bills were stacking up. But her mother didn't want her racing at all. Let alone for another stable—and on a *weekday.*

The arguments chasing each other around her brain made her want to go back to bed and pull the covers over her head.

SHE HATED FIGHTING!

So, she needed to apologize to her mother and ask for forgiveness. That's just as bad. The thoughts were a flock of scavenger crows tearing her peace of mind to pieces.

"I'll drop you off at school on my way to the track." David joined the family at the breakfast table. For a change Trish wasn't grabbing peanut butter toast on the run.

"I'll be ready in five minutes." She set her cereal bowl in the sink, then went back to the table where Marge sat drinking a cup of coffee. "Mom, I'm sorry I yelled at you last night. I . . ."

"Me, too." Marge drew her daughter into the circle

of her arm and hugged her. "Have a good day. And Trish, I *am* proud of you."

"Thanks, Mom. Give Dad a hug for me. When do you think he'll be home?"

"Probably Wednesday afternoon."

"Oh." Trish nodded. The hand of fear grabbing her throat kept her from saying anything else. "Gotta run. See ya."

What was she going to do? Halfway to school she turned to David. "I need a favor, big brother."

"What now? More chemistry?"

"No. I need a ride to the track on Wednesday right after school."

"What for?"

"To ride for Rodgers. He asked me on Sunday after he was so pleased with the race. He wanted me to ride twice but one was during school. This one's about four."

"Have you asked Mom and Dad?"

"No. But we need the money."

David shook his head. "Trish, I won't lie for you."

"It's not exactly a lie ... just not telling them everything."

David shot her one of his big-brother looks. "You better call Rodgers and tell him you can't."

"Thanks for nothing." Trish opened the door when the pickup stopped at the curb. "You're all heart."

Now, what do I do? she thought as she crossed the wide sidewalk to the school entrance.

Shock stopped her dead in her tracks as she stepped through the doorway. A computer banner, the block letters filled in with crimson and gold, said:

"Way to go, Trish. On to the Derby." The banner stretched from post to post. Another sign hid half the trophy case.

All the way to her locker, students congratulated her. Even the principal said congratulations when he passed her in the hall. Another sign, this one announcing #1 Jockey, taped her locker closed.

Rhonda leaned against her own locker. "So, what do you think?"

Trish just shook her head. "You guys are awesome." She carefully removed the taped sign so she could get into her locker, and folded it to save. "You must have spent all night on this stuff."

"I had lots of help. In fact, it was Doug's idea."

Trish blinked. "Come on."

Rhonda nodded. "Yup." She leaned real close. "I think he likes you."

The funny glow in Trish's middle stayed through the day. So many kids stopped by their table at lunchtime that Brad threatened to eat somewhere else—in peace. And when Trish aced a chemistry quiz she felt like she'd used her eagle's wings to top a mountain.

When the final bell rang, she took the sign from the shelf in her locker, grabbed the books she needed and headed for Brad's Mustang.

The Runnin' On Farm pickup was parked at the curb, motor idling. David pushed open the door. "Hustle, Trish. There's trouble at the track."

CHAPTER 5

"What happened?" Trish tossed her books in the cab.

"Spitfire threw Genie. He's gone crazy. Won't even let me near him."

"Is he hurt?" Trish slammed the door behind her.

"No! Just nuts!"

"Where is he?"

"We got him back in his stall. But he still has the bridle and saddle on. I dropped Genie off at the hospital to have her shoulder X-rayed. She's hurting pretty bad."

"Have you talked to Dad yet?"

"Yeah." David cruised through a yellow light. "He said to get you, and get that crazy horse home tonight if we can. Who knows when Genie can ride again."

Trish shook her head. "You better slow down, a ticket isn't going to help us any."

David let up on the gas but shot her a dirty look.

"Hey, it's not my fault. If they'd just let me work the horses like we're all used to, things would be fine."

"Yeah, and if Dad wasn't sick, I'd be in Pullman and not worrying about all this . . . this stuff. I'm not a trainer. How're we gonna load him?"

"Spitfire'll behave for me." Trish chewed on the inside of her cheek.

"You better hope so. You didn't see him go crazy like I did."

"Let's bring Gatesby home, too," Trish continued as if she hadn't heard him. "Dad'll know of someone else to work the other two. They're easy to manage."

Trish leaped from the truck as soon as it stopped at the racing stables.

"Be careful, Trish," David hollered after her as she sprinted to Spitfire's stall. Both halves of the door were closed. A rapid tatoo of hooves on the wall and an high-pitched scream left no doubt that Spitfire hadn't forgotten the incident.

"Hey, fella, easy now. You know better than to act like this." Trish slid back the bolt on the top half of the door. A hoof slammed against the wall again. "Come on, Spitfire. This is me. I'm gonna open the door and let some light in." Trish followed her words with actions. Spitfire whinnied, but the sound was more greeting than anger.

As the light hit him, he tossed his head, ears laid flat. The bit jangled. His nostrils flared so wide they glowed red in the dimness. The whites of his eyes glimmered against his black hide.

"You've really made a mess of things, haven't you?" Trish leaned on the stall door. She kept her tone low and her body relaxed, as if nothing were wrong.

Spitfire exhaled, the whuffle sound blowing through his lips. He shook his head, his forelock brushing from side to side. After an all-over shake that set the stirrups clapping against his sides, his ears pricked forward. The colt stretched to sniff Trish's proffered hand and blew again, as if letting out all the tension. Finally he stepped forward to drape his head over Trish's shoulder.

"Good boy," Trish rubbed behind his ears and down the arched neck. Dried lather and sweat crusted his fine black coat. A raw spot on his lower lip from fighting the bit hadn't had time to scab over. Spitfire trembled when Trish opened the lower door and stepped inside the stall. "Let's get this bridle off." She worked as she talked and slipped the web halter back over his nose. As soon as the colt was cross-tied, she checked his legs for swelling.

"Want some help?" David asked from the door.

Spitfire laid back his ears and stamped one fore-foot.

"No, let me get him cleaned up and calmed down. Then we'll see. How're the others?" Trish removed the saddle and slung it over the stall door.

"Gatesby missed me today but bit Genie a good one, so he's about normal. Genie worked all three of them before she and Spitfire got into it."

As David and Trish talked, she could feel Spitfire relaxing. She brushed while she spoke, finishing one side and moving around to the other.

"She sure has that touch," Trish heard someone say to David outside the stall. "I wouldn't a'gone in there with that black for nothin'."

"He really put on a show," another voice chimed in. "How's Stokes?"

"I don't know." The voices faded away.

Trish finished grooming Spitfire and went to the

tackroom for tape to wrap his legs. She hung up the saddle and bridle and dug a handful of grain out of the bin.

On the way back, she stopped at Dan'l's stall. The gray nickered and rubbed his forehead against her shoulder. As he lipped the grain from her hand, Trish rubbed his ears and the poll of his head. "You old sweety, you'd never do anything like that, would you?" Dan'l's eyes closed in bliss. "You don't get nearly enough attention here." Trish dropped a kiss on his nose and went back to working with Spitfire.

The black rested his weight on three legs so a rear one could be bent and relaxed completely. His head drooped as far as the crossties allowed. Eyes closed, he slept, worn out from all the excitement.

What a change, Trish thought as she leaned on the door. *You just don't like another rider, do you? I didn't realize how much you are my horse.*

"But you know," she continued her thoughts aloud as she swung open the door, "you've got to let another jockey ride you, just in case something happens to me sometime." Spitfire shook his head. Trish chuckled as she squatted to firmly wrap the white tape from fetlock to just below the knee.

"The trailer's here." David kept his voice soft, but Spitfire flicked his ears.

"Okay. We're ready. Come on in and take one of the ties so we both have hold of him."

As David entered the stall the colt raised his head. David held out a palm of grain. Spitfire munched happily, as if the day's events had never happened. He whuffled, then licked David's hand for the salt.

"You coulda behaved like this earlier, you know."
He rubbed the droopy black face and ears. David unclipped the ropes and handed one to Trish. Spitfire
thumped his way into the trailer without even a
glance at the other activities in the area.

"Let's get Gatesby. We'll walk him double-tied
too." Trish knotted the lead ropes with a bow that
could be pulled loose with just a jerk on the end of the
rope. She patted Spitfire on the rump as she pushed
him over so she could get out. "*Thank you*, God," she
breathed as she strode down the ramp.

Gatesby nickered a greeting. His black ears
touched at the tips they were pricked so far forward.
When Trish reached for his halter, he rolled his eyes
and tipped his head sideways, ready to nip.

"Knock it off!" Trish clipped the lead ropes to the
halter ring while David held the opposite side of the
halter. "You just have to get your licks in, don't you?"
Gatesby dropped his head, asking for an ear rub. Trish
obliged, all the while keeping a wary eye for any shenanigans.

Gatesby stepped smartly out of the stall when David swung open the lower door. Ears flicking to catch
all sounds, including Trish's comforting voice, he ambled between them; until his front feet thudded on the
trailer gate.

The ropes burned through their hands as the bay
lunged backward.

"Oh, for Pete's sake!" Trish clutched the remaining
rope in her hand. "You've done this before." As one,
she and David jerked their lead lines. Gatesby shook
his head. Trish smacked him on the nose as his front

feet started to leave the ground. "Now behave your-self!" The bay shook all over and pricked his ears again. When he blew in her face, Trish shook her head and led him forward. This time he thumped his way into the trailer with laid-back ears.

"Ow-w!" Trish yelped. She slapped the bay's shoulder. "Get off my foot!" The sneaky look on Gatesby's face told Trish he'd stepped deliberately. She shoved against his shoulder to force him to move over and limped out of the trailer. "One of these days you're gonna be dog food," she muttered as she pulled off her boot and massaged her toes.

David slammed the tailgate in place. "Let's feed so we can get outta here."

"Easy for you to say, you can walk." Trish flexed her foot.

Both horses seemed glad to get home when Trish and David led them to their stalls. The workout passed without a hitch, but by the time all the animals were fed, dusk had deepened into darkness. Trish spent a few precious minutes playing with Miss Tee before she limped up the rise to the dark house.

The message light flashed on the phone when she walked into the house. Bob Diego had two mounts for her the next day. Trish called him back. "I'd love to," she said.

That night in bed the argument took over her mind again. One side demanded, *You've got to tell your parents about the mounts on Wednesday.* The other side blasted back, *You can't. They'll never let you ride.* "But we've got to have the money!" Trish turned her pillow over and smashed it with her fist. There was no insurance. She'd heard her mom and dad discussing the medical bills. The hospital had eaten up their savings just like the cancer ate up her father's body. And they had no income. Her dad wasn't training enough horses. That only left the purses they won and her percentage as a jockey.

But you HAVE to tell them, her nagging voice intruded. *You can't lie, you know you can't. And besides, how are you going to get to the track?*

Trish flipped onto her back and locked her hands behind her head. When she tried praying, the words seemed to bounce off the ceiling and fade like falling stars on a clear night.

Well, God. She took a deep breath. *You promised to take care of us, but as far as I can see, you're not doing too good a job.* She paused, an idea tiptoeing into her mind. *Maybe my being offered mounts is God's way of taking care of us.* She grinned with satisfaction as she turned on her side. *Of course!* She ignored the muttering of her nagger as sleep hit her like a sledgehammer.

———

David had broken all speed records to get her to class before the bell. She hadn't even had time to stop at her locker, just run from the car to class in spite of her sore foot.

Spitfire hadn't been feeling too well that morning either. There was some swelling in his front leg and tenderness in a rear hock where he'd probably banged himself in all the ruckus.

"Serves you right." Trish had scolded him. All she

needed was a lame horse right now.

The lunch bell rang before she saw Brad. She leaned her forehead against her locker. The cool metal eased the pressure she felt building behind her eyes.

"Now what?" Brad stopped beside her.

"More problems."

"Is it your dad?"

"No . . . yes . . . well, sort of."

"That tells me a lot."

"Come on, you guys." Rhonda joined them. "The food'll be all gone." The look on Trish's face stopped her. "Now what?"

"I've been asked to ride in two races tomorrow afternoon."

"Wow! That's great." Rhonda looked from Trish to Brad, who shrugged his shoulders.

"But you know what Mom's said about riding."

"Yeah, that's right." Rhonda paused. "So what are you gonna do?"

"Ask Brad to take me to the track."

"Naturally." Brad shook his head. "What did David say?"

"Plenty. But the bottom line was no way." Trish raised her head, her jaw clenched tight. "I *have* to get there. I gave my word . . ." Her voice dropped to a whisper. "And we need the money."

Brad rubbed his forehead with one tanned hand. "I'll take you," he said finally. "But I think you should talk this over with your dad first."

"I can't. What if he says no?" Trish started down the hall. "Are you guys coming or what?" She walked backwards so she could watch her friends catch up to her. "Thanks."

"So. When *are* you going to tell your dad?" Rhonda asked as they entered the lunchroom.

"Not till I have to, I guess."

CHAPTER 6

Study Halls are usually intended for studying.

What a joke! Trish felt like smashing her books to the floor. *I can't study today.* She stared out the window. The Oregon liquid-sunshine misted the trees at the corners of the quad. The dismal outside matched her dismal inside. *I'll just have to tell them I have something after school tomorrow.*

But that's a lie! Her nagger wriggled out from under his rock.

Trish pushed her fingers through her bangs. *I can't help that.*

You'll be sorry.

So, what's new? I already am. But I have *to ride. We need the money.*

What if you lose?

Trish's pencil lead snapped against her paper. *That* hadn't entered her mind before. She slid from behind her desk and headed for the pencil sharpener. She glanced at the clock. *Five minutes till the bell. What a relief.*

———

At Runnin' On Farm, wind blew the drizzle into

sheets that drifted across the track during the afternoon workout. While her windbreaker provided some protection, it failed to prevent icy water from dripping down the back of her neck. Her nose ran faster than the horses.

She pulled the saddle off Gatesby and slung it over the door. "Good job, fella." The pat on his neck spoke more warmly than the words. Gatesby shook; drops from his mane spattered her face. "Way to go."

"I'll finish here." David set down his bucket with scraper and water. "You go on up and get warm."

Trish nodded. "You need me any more?"

"Nah. I'm almost done. Mom wants us to come to the hospital for dinner."

"Okay. But we can't stay long. I've got a ton of homework."

———

"You're awfully quiet, Tee." Hal leaned forward in his wheelchair. The four of them sat around a small table in the hospital cafeteria. They'd already discussed the horses both at the track and home.

Trish took a deep breath. "I . . . ah . . ."

Tell him! her nagger commanded; the voice so loud in her ears she was afraid her father had heard it.

"Ah . . . when are you coming home?"

"Not till Friday, it looks like. I think the doctor likes having me here." Hal smiled. "Think I'll start charging him for the racing tips."

Trish grinned at him. "Yeah, I think you better. Make your fees as much as his." She pushed herself to her feet. "Come on David, let's hit the road. My books are waiting."

"I'll be home soon," Marge said.

"Bye, Dad." Trish hugged her father. Instead of the usual horses and hay, he smelled like hospital. That old familiar boulder blocked her throat. And he was so thin. His navy blue robe hung on his bony shoulders. "Get better."

"I love you, Tee," he whispered in her ear.

Don't say that! she almost screamed the thought as she left the room. *God, when are you going to make him better?*

Trish felt the load lift from her shoulders as she walked down the hall. Friday—he wouldn't be home until Friday. Now she wouldn't need to lie.

———

The next day flew by. Trish felt like someone had cranked up her treadmill to sprinting speed. She'd packed boots and helmet in her duffel bag and told David it was some stuff for Rhonda. She'd lied after all, but at least not to her parents.

"You're sure you want to do this?" Brad asked when she slid into the front seat of his Mustang.

"Too late to back out now. Those owners are counting on me. Where's Rhonda?"

"She took the bus home."

"At least it quit raining." Trish broke the long silence on the drive to Portland. Butterflies took turns doing aerial flips in her midsection.

"But the track may still be muddy. Trish . . ." Brad turned to face his friend as she opened the car door.

He'd stopped right in front of the gate closest to the dressing rooms.

"It's okay, Brad. I'll be careful." She paused and stuck her head back in the door. "Meet me here right after the seventh race, okay? I've gotta gallop Spitfire and Gatesby as soon as I can get home."

"Are you Tricia Evanston?" A young man in a black windbreaker asked just as she reached the locker room.

"Yes."

"Here're your silks. Bob'll meet you in the paddock as soon as you're dressed." He handed her the shiny black and white shirt and helmet cover.

"Okay. Thanks." Trish took the hanger and pushed open the door. The now-familiar, liniment-scented steam tickled her nose. Even though this was only the fourth race of the day, the room had already adopted the cluttered look. It reminded Trish of her own room. Except for the smell.

"How's Genie?" she asked one of the other jockeys.

"Should be back by the weekend. Good thing she only dislocated that shoulder rather than pullin' the muscles or breakin' it." The jockey twisted her long blond hair and pinned it on top of her head. "You're Tricia Evanston, right?"

Trish nodded.

"And it was your horse that threw her?"

"Yeah. Spitfire doesn't seem to like anyone else on his back. I didn't know he was such a one-person horse. Sure sorry Genie got hurt."

"Happens to the best of us." The woman settled her helmet in place. "You take care now."

The brief conversation left Trish feeling both bad about Spitfire and happy Genie was okay. She would take care . . . but she needed the win.

This time she hadn't met the horse before the race. While she knew her father's advice was sound, she also understood that pre-meets weren't always possible.

Her mount had drawn the number five position. Right in the middle of the pack. Robert Diego stood to the side of the trainer as Trish entered the stall.

"Good afternoon." His voice had the precise inflection of one to whom English was a second language. "Permit me to give you a leg up."

Trish smiled at him. "I'd like to meet your horse first, if that's okay?"

Diego nodded, a smile tugging at the corners of his mouth. "Be my guest. This old man here is called Hospitality, otherwise known as Hoppy. He's five years old, won some, lost more, and back after an injury in California. He likes to come from behind, but is never pleased with a muddy track."

Trish stood quietly in front of the leggy blood-red bay and let him explore first her hands, her arms and up to her helmet. His breath in her face signified approval and she extended a hand to rub along his head and up to his ears. He had the chiseled bones and large eyes of a mature horse, not the teen-age look of her own string. She brushed his forelock aside and rubbed between his ears.

"You've made a friend for life," Diego said. "He doesn't usually take to newcomers quite so easily."

Trish listened hard to the trainer's reply, trying to pick out words she knew from the rapid Spanish. *Muy bueno* she knew meant very good.

Trish mounted and settled herself in the saddle. So he didn't like mud. Well, he'd get a lot of that today if they came from behind.

Hoppy tugged against the bit as they filed on the post parade. Trish rose in her stirrups, testing his mouth, feeling him bunch under her. His ears twitched in perfect time to her sing-song.

As they entered the gates, she stroked Hoppy's arched neck. His ears pricked forward. He blew, tensed for the shot, and exploded from the gate. Within four strides he broke ahead of the pack and leaped for the first curve.

Trish crouched over his shoulders, giving him all the encouragement she could while keeping a firm hand on the reins. She didn't want him to tire before the stretch, but he was running with his head up. He tested the bit, lengthening his stride when she relaxed even a little.

As the marker poles flashed past, Trish listened for her competition. At the three-quarters point the pair running a length behind made their move. With hooves thundering up on both sides of her, she loosed the reins. Her mount's surge of power carried him another length ahead. He seemed to be laughing as they crossed the finish line two lengths ahead of the mud-covered, second-place contender.

"So you don't like mud in your face, eh, Hoppy?" Trish laughed as she pulled him down to a canter. "And you like to come from behind. Sure fooled me." She turned him back toward the winner's circle. "And your owner."

"Sorry, Mr. Diego," she said as she slid to the ground. "Keeping him back when he'd broken so clean just didn't seem the right thing to do. And he was having too much fun in front."

Bob Diego smiled and nodded but Trish could feel his black eyes assessing her.

He'll probably never ask me again, since I didn't follow his directions. She snapped her goggles up to her helmet. *But I just knew what the horse wanted. And needed. And we won.*

After the trainer led Hospitality away to the testing barn, Trish fell in step with Bob Diego as he spoke. "You have the insight, that special gift, do you not?" He rubbed his chin between forefinger and thumb.

"Wha . . . what do you mean?"

"It's rare. That ability to get the best out of a horse. Some say they can read the horse's mind or else the horse can read theirs. Whichever. It is not important how, but that you can."

Trish took a deep breath. "I don't know, Mr. Diego. About the gift, I mean. I always thought it was only because I was around our animals so much; they know me and I know them. But your horse today . . . well, I'm just glad I didn't make a mistake."

Robert Diego nodded. "Now, about this next race."

———

Trish could feel the explosive energy of the colt she mounted next. He fought her all the way to the post and back to the starting gate. "Now, if you think you can get away with all this, you're crazy," she instructed his twitching ears. "I ride Gatesby and you don't have a chance on winning the sneakiness trophy next to him. Settle down. Your time is coming."

When they entered the gate, the colt snorted and reared. Trish backed him out and walked him in a tight circle, all the while using her voice and hands to calm the fractious beast. "You're wasting your energy," she commanded. "Now just behave and let's get on the other side so you can run."

She felt him relax. They stopped for just a moment, time for both of them to expel a deep breath. This time he settled for the break, his weight on his haunches as it should be.

This was the first time Trish and her mount were caught in the middle of the pack. As they rounded the first turn, she pulled him back and out of the box of surging horseflesh and swinging bats. The colt shook his head at the restriction but settled again at the sound of her voice.

She could hear Bob Diego's voice in her ear. "I like my horses to come from the rear. Save them for the stretch, then use the whip if you have to."

First one, then another horse dropped back as they rounded the far turn. The pace had been stiff but when Trish let up on the reins, the colt extended his stride. He was running easily, ears flicking both to hear his rider and to look forward.

With the final two horses neck and neck in front of them, Trish let the colt have his head, her hands on the reins to support, not control him. They swept across the wire, winning by half a length.

"You did it!" She felt like hugging the prancing horse. *And no whip.* The thought brought a grin of satisfaction. The other two jockeys had laid on the whips for all they were worth, but her mount won.

They posed for the pictures and Trish gave the colt one last pat. "Congratulations." Diego shook her hand. "That one, he gave you a hard time at first, no?"

"We had a bit of a discussion about who was boss. Guess I convinced him we should work together." Trish stepped off the scale and handed the saddle to the trainer. She wiped a chunk of track off her cheek. "But coming from behind on a muddy track . . . well."

The owner laughed. "I have one tomorrow in the fourth. Can you ride for me again?"

"Sure."

"He's a problem sometimes. Seems to do better with a woman on him. This will be his third race, but he's never won. If he doesn't at least show, I'll enter him in a claiming race next."

"I'll do my best."

"Here." His smile gleamed beneath a well-trimmed mustache, as the man handed Trish an envelope. "Tell your father he's done a good job, both as a trainer . . . and as a father."

"Th—thanks," Trish stammered her surprise. *If he only knew.*

Jason Rogers joined her in the winner's circle after Trish rode his horse to win also. It had been an excellent day, if only she could tell her dad about it.

Even though Trish changed clothes as fast as she could and Brad drove more than the speed limit, it was dark when they turned at the Runnin' On Farm sign.

"You want me to ride Gatsby?" Brad asked as

they trotted down to the stables. The dark house and vacant drive had given Trish a brief relief. No one else was home yet.

"No, I better. Just help me saddle up. David must be at the hospital yet, so if you'd feed it would sure help."

Trish had just dismounted from her final circuit when David stomped up. "How come you're so late? You should have been done hours ago. What's been going on?"

Anger and guilt clipped each word as Trish turned on her brother. "Who made you my boss?"

CHAPTER 7

"Where were you?"

"Where do you think?" Trish faced him—hands on her hips, her jaw tight and eyes flashing.

"You rode after all."

"You bet I did. We *need* the money, haven't you figured that out yet?"

"How . . . who. . . ?"

"Who cares? I rode and I won. Someone in this family has to be making some money. You know how much everything costs. And I didn't miss school."

"No, but you lied to Mom and Dad." David grabbed her arm.

"No, I didn't. They didn't ask and I didn't say anything. But I could have had another mount if I had skipped. Dad says to use my gift and I am." Trish whirled away. "I'm doing the best I can, David, so leave me alone."

"All right! I will! Just don't come crying to me when they find out."

"Yes, *Mother*."

"You're not funny."

"Oh, r-e-a-l-l-y. You're so bossy. Think you always know what's best."

"Stupid kid."

"Takes one to know one." Trish couldn't believe they were hollering at each other like this. She and David never fought. But right now she felt she could strangle him with her bare hands. Calling her stupid. All the feelings of guilt and resentment rushed up from her toes and erupted.

"Leave me alone, David Lee Evanston!" she yelled. "If you know what's good for you."

"And what'll you do about it, if I don't?" Red flamed up into David's face. His fists bunched at his sides, ready to punch. Instead of at her, he slammed one fist against the barn wall.

Trish froze. Tears welled behind her eyes, clogged her throat and spilled down her cheeks.

David grunted with the pain. He doubled over, cushioning his injured hand with the other.

"David, I . . . I'm sorry." Trish put her hand on his shoulder.

David stepped back. "Haven't you done enough?" Clamping his hand against his chest, he headed for the house.

Brad held Trish while she cried. As the deluge dried to drips, she pulled away and wiped her eyes on her sleeve. "I just don't know what else to do," she finally muttered. "We need the money. Dad'll understand."

"When are you going to tell him?"

"When he gets home, so we can talk by ourselves." She drew another shuddering breath. "Well, I better get at the horses." She looked around, as if coming into new territory from a far land.

"I put them all away."

"Thanks."

"We need to feed. I don't think David will be back down."

"I know. Hope he's icing that hand." Trish chewed her lip. "Do you think he broke anything?"

"You're lucky he didn't break you."

Trish nodded. Her deep breath snagged on a clump of tears still stuck in her throat. "I'll do grain and you get the hay." She felt like a ton of alfalfa sat on her shoulders. If she didn't start moving, her knees would buckle under the load, and once she went down, how would she ever get up?

————————

David's door was shut when she finally got up to the dark house. She warmed two bowls of leftover spaghetti in the microwave, buttered some French bread and poured two glasses of milk. After arranging all the food on a tray, Trish carried it down the hall and tapped on David's door.

"Yeah."

"I've brought dinner." She bent one knee to balance the tray and struggled with the doorknob. Almost upsetting the milk, she kicked the door open with her foot. "Whew, that was close."

Only the clock dial glowed in the darkened room. Light from the hall showed David huddled on the bed, facing the opposite wall.

Trish set the tray down on the desk and switched on the lamp. "David, I'm sorry for hollering at you like that."

"Yeah." He flinched when he tried to push himself against the headboard. "Me too."

Trish could tell he'd been crying. Was he feeling as wretched as she was? Did he ever get mad at God and the cancer like she did? If so, he never said anything about it. Was he mad that he didn't get to go back for his second year in college? If only she dared ask him all these questions.

"Here's your dinner," she said instead, handing him the bowl and bread. "I'll get some ice for your hand."

As she wrapped the ice bag in a towel to hold it in place, she asked, "Do you think anything's broken?"

David shook his head. "No."

"What's Mom gonna say?"

"I'll just tell her it was an accident." He spilled some spaghetti on his shirt.

Any other time Trish would have giggled at the look of disgust on his face. Her neat-nick brother didn't spill. But then he hadn't had to eat left-handed before.

"David," Trish paused, trying to choose the best words. "About the racing . . ." She met his gaze, not willing to back down. "I . . . I wouldn't have done it if we didn't need the money so bad. It's just like other kids who have jobs after school."

"Yeah, but other kids have their parents' permission."

"I know. And other kids don't make near the money I do."

"That has nothing to do . . ."

"With it? Yeah it does. For us it does." She picked

up the empty dishes. "I'm not gonna race forever—without permission, I mean. I'll talk to Dad as soon as he gets home."

"Are you going to ride again?"

She nodded. "Tomorrow."

———

"You racing again?" Rhonda asked at the lunch table.

"Um-mmm," Trish mumbled around a bite of tuna salad. "You want to come with me? You could help exercise in the evening, too. Gatesby needs a rider, and it's so late when I get home."

"Okay. I've a show this weekend, so I won't be jumping tonight." She picked up her tray to leave. "You told your mom and dad yet?"

Trish shook her head. "Dad's coming home Friday. I'll tell him then."

"Hard, huh?"

"Yeah. I've always told him everything. Last night David and I really got into it. I've felt like screaming at anything . . . and everybody. Or crying. But if I start, how'll I ever stop? The only time I ever feel good any more is when I'm on a horse."

———

Trish really felt good after the first race. Another win. The horse exploded under her in the backstretch and they won by two furlongs. Mr. Diego slipped her an envelope with $50 in it. That was on top of her share of the purse.

Her second mount was for Rodgers Ranch, so she

changed silks quickly. She was ready when the trainer brought a gray gelding into the saddling paddock.

"Hey, you look like Dan'l," she waited for the horse to finish inspecting her. "He's one of my best buddies." She kept up a flow of conversation while she stroked the horse's neck and head.

"Dundee's been racing for three years," Rodgers said when he joined them. "He had a bad spill last season and strained his shoulder, so this is his first time out again."

Trish listened carefully to the instructions, but her hands never ceased their stroking and rubbing, communicating her care for the horse. Her favorite fragrance filled her nose—horse, along with dust and saddle leather.

The noise of the crowd faded into the background, replaced by jangling bits, stomping hooves, and the sharp whinny of a high-strung contender.

The gray blew in her face, his breath warm and damp. Trish mounted, feeling like she and the horse were already one. The gray settled deep on his haunches as the gate clanged shut. Trish stroked his neck one more time, the thrill of the moment tingling through both of them.

Dundee broke clean, but within four strides was trapped in the middle of the field. The only alternative was to pull back, away from the surging haunches in front and around them. Just as Trish tightened the reins, Dundee stumbled, clipped by another horse.

Trish instinctively held his head up, using all her strength and determination to keep the animal on his feet. He faltered. Stumbled again.

"Come on, Dundee," Trish pleaded. "You can do it." By the time he regained his footing, the field had left them a furlong behind.

Dundee straightened out again, ears laid back. Each stride and heave of his mighty haunches hurled them closer to the trailing pack. One by one, he passed the spread-out field. By the stretch he inched up on the third-place rider. Trish rode high over his shoulders, giving him every advantage.

"Come on, Dundee, you can do it." She felt him reach further. He settled deeper, intent as they pulled into second place. They caught the front runner by the last furlong pole. Nose to tail, nose to haunches, nose to neck.

The other jockey went to the whip.

They flew across the finish line stride on stride.

"And that's number four to win and three to place," the announcer's voice could barely be heard over the heaving of her mount.

"Sorry, boy, you gave it all you had. If the race had been even three yards longer, you'd a made it." Trish pulled him down to a slow gallop, then an easy canter as she swung back to the exit gate. Dundee pricked his ears and tossed his head.

"Some race, Trish." Jason Rodgers met her at the weighing platform. "I thought for sure he was going to go down, but you kept him on his feet."

"Sorry we didn't win." Trish stepped on the scale. "But that horse is all heart. He gave it everything he had, we just ran out of track."

"I know." Rodgers slipped her an envelope. "You earned it," he said at her surprised look. "And I have a mount for you Saturday, and one on Sunday."

"I'll have to check what races we're in."

"I already did. Thanks, Trish." He started to leave. "Oh, and say Hi to your dad for me. Tell him thanks for raising such a promising jockey."

"Thank you, Mr. Rodgers." Trish waved as the tall man strode off.

"Are you Tricia Evanston?" A voice by her side brought her back.

"Yes."

"Come on, Trish." Rhonda handed Trish her bag. "Brad's got the car waiting outside the gate."

"Okay. Okay." She turned to the slender woman who'd asked her name. "I've gotta hurry."

"I'll walk you out. How many races have you won now?" The woman fell into step beside Rhonda and Trish.

"Uh . . ." Trish counted in her head. "Six, I think."

"And how long have you been racing?"

"A couple of weeks."

"Why do you think you're doing so well?"

"I just seem to understand the horses, I guess," Trish said. "You a jockey?"

"No, I'm a . . ."

"Come on, Trish," Brad hollered. "It's gonna be dark soon."

"Sorry, I gotta run." Trish dashed across the gravel to Brad's car.

"Who was that?" Brad asked as he drove out of the parking lot.

"Beats me." Trish and Rhonda both shrugged.

When Trish settled deeper into the seat, the words

of Jason Rodgers came into her mind. *His compliment sure felt good.* She pulled the envelope from her pocket and opened it. "A hundred dollars!" She swiveled in the seat to stare at Rhonda.

"Wow!" Rhonda grinned at the sight of the five $20 bills. "Hey, there's a note too."

Trish read it aloud. "I know things are tight right now for all of you. Hope this helps a little. Thanks. Jason Rodgers." Trish felt the sting of tears behind her eyes. What a wonderful thing for him to do. If only she could show the note to her father right now.

At least she wouldn't be visiting him tonight. It was hard enough to keep the information from him when they spoke on the phone. *I never knew lying could take so much time and energy,* she thought. *What a mess I've gotten into.*

———

The next afternoon Trish flew into the house. All the family cars lined the driveway. "Dad?" She dumped her books on the counter and headed for the living room. "Wow! It's so good to have you home."

Her father raised his recliner with a thump. There was no smile on his face. His arms remained at his sides.

Trish dropped to her knees beside the chair. "Dad?" her voice squeaked.

Hal handed her the sports section of the local newspaper. The headline read: "Local Girl Rides To Win."

CHAPTER 8

So much for a happy homecoming.

Trish skimmed the first paragraph, and knew. The photo of her and Bob Diego in the winner's circle was a dead give away, one she couldn't argue with. She kept her eyes on the paper, but rather than read the rest of the copy, her brain scrambled for an out.

"Well?" Her father prodded.

"I was going to tell you as soon as you got home." Trish dropped the paper on the hearth and straightened her shoulders. She could feel the tears gathering at the back of her throat. She swallowed—hard. No crying this time.

"All I'll say now, Tricia . . ."

She swallowed again. It had been a long time since her father used her full name, and in such a stern voice.

". . . is that I'm—we're," he took her mother's hand, "disappointed, deeply disappointed, in what you've done. I know you have to load those horses, so we'll discuss this when you get home. Understood?"

Trish nodded. One glance at her mother's flashing eyes and rigid jaw warned her that the discussion would *not* be comfortable. Trish looked at her father

81

again. He'd leaned back in the recliner, eyes closed, as if he didn't want to look at her.

Trish ran from the room before the tears spilled over. *She would not let them see her cry.*

David had an I-warned-you look about him when she got down to the stables. He'd already backed the trailer in place for loading.

Trish leaned against Spitfire, both arms around his neck. The colt bobbed his head and rubbed his chin against her back. With her cheek against his mane, she breathed in the comforting odor of warm horse-flesh. The quiet stalls, except for Gatesby rustling straw in the adjoining box, offered her the peace of mind she needed to handle the hours ahead. Trish took a deep breath. *Well, Dad. I did the best I could. I guess— no, I know I should have gone to you first, but I didn't. All I can say is, I'm sorry.* With the decision made, she clipped the lead to Spitfire's halter and led him out and into the trailer.

"Want help with Gatesby?" David asked.

Trish nodded.

Ears flat, Gatesby threw up his head when she reached for his halter. "Oh, knock it off," she ordered as she reached again, this time clamping firm fingers around the blue webbing. "We don't need any trouble from you today."

David snapped a lead rope on the opposite side as she paused before leading the colt out the opened stall door. Gatesby jumped around, rolling his eyes and spooking at anything that moved, including shadows. But at the echo of front feet on the trailer gate, he lunged backward. The bay planted his feet like trees.

No matter what they tried—grain, a carrot, kind words—the horse wouldn't budge.

When David got behind Gatesby to push, the horse lashed out with one rear hoof, barely missing David's knee.

David muttered some words Trish knew he hadn't learned at home.

Gatesby glared at Trish. He even pulled away when she stroked his neck and rubbed the spot behind his ear.

"I'm hooding him." David stalked off to the tack room.

"You dummy." Trish felt the urge to smack the stubborn horse with her whip. "You could use a whip right now, and we don't even keep one down here at the barn."

Gatesby shivered when David slipped the hood in place. He dropped his head and sighed, a deep sigh that melted all resistance, then followed his two leaders into the trailer.

Trish wisely kept her mouth shut. The look on David's face matched the one she'd seen earlier on her father's.

———————

By the time they'd unloaded the horses and fed all the stock, darkness blanketed the landscape. A drizzle blew in on the evening wind. David decided to cut the workout, so Trish gave Dan'l an extra bit of rubbing attention before they unhitched the trailer and headed for home.

"I'm starved." Trish stuffed her cold hands in her

pockets. "Let's stop at Mac's for a burger."

David obligingly took the roads to I–5 and stopped at the drive-through window. With Coke and hamburger in hand, David completed the circular on-ramp back to the freeway. Traffic ground to a halt, and flashing signs overhead announced the raising of the bridge to allow a ship to pass up or down the Columbia River.

"Sorry." Trish hid behind her Coke. The glare David cast her way was enough to melt the ice in her drink.

Maybe Dad'll be asleep by the time we get home. Trish allowed that and other dreamy thoughts to occupy her mind. They were better than those of her nagger. She'd heard enough from him the last few days to last a lifetime.

Just tell the truth, and I'll let . . . It was her nagger again, getting in his nickel's worth. Trish tried to concentrate on Saturday's race.

"Sure hope Gatesby settles down by tomorrow." She slurped the last bit of soft drink.

"Hmm-mm." David settled further down in the seat. He finished his food and thrummed his fingers on the steering wheel.

Trish jabbed her straw to the swish of the windshield wipers. All she could think about was the confrontation ahead.

David grabbed the container out of her hand. "For Pete's sake . . ."

"Sor-ry."

Traffic began moving again.

"David?"

"Yeah."

"What do you think they're gonna do?"

"Mom and Dad? I don't know. They're both hurt and mad."

"And disappointed."

"Yeah."

Trish chewed on her lip. "What do you think I should do?"

"Just get it over with. You want to be treated like an adult, here's your chance to act like one."

Trish settled lower in the seat.

———

When she arrived home, Caesar greeted her, then followed David to the barn where he'd finish the evening chores. The fire crackling in the fireplace was warm and inviting when Trish opened the sliding glass door. The fish tank bubbled comfortingly in the corner. She pulled off her boots at the jack and shrugged out of her jacket. She could see her father lying in the recliner, his eyes closed. Her mother's rocking chair sang its familiar creaky tune.

Trish took a deep breath.

"There's dinner in the oven." Marge didn't look up from her knitting.

"Thanks. I'm not hungry." Trish crossed the room to sit on the fieldstone hearth. "Is Dad . . ."

"I'm awake, Tee. Just start at the beginning."

"Well, last Sunday Mr. Rodgers asked me to ride for him on Wednesday. I told him yes before I even thought because I was so happy to be asked. Then I . . ." Trish told everything she could think of, including her load of guilt. "And I'm sorry for lying—not telling you all the truth. But Dad, I know how bad we need the money." She studied her hands hanging between her knees. Neither of her parents had said a word the entire time.

When she sneaked a look at her mother, Trish could see the still-tight jaw. Her knitting needles seemed to jab into the yarn.

"Well . . . why don't you holler at me—anything. Say something!" She dropped to her knees beside her father's chair. "Please, Dad, I'm so sorry." The tears came, silently dripping onto her hands that clenched the recliner arm.

Her father lifted a hand and stroked her bent head. "Trish, this hasn't been easy for any of us. But we've trusted you kids to be honest with us. You broke that trust."

"But I . . . I . . ." Trish tried to talk around the tears.

"I know. You did the best you could. And you did a good job, but the bottom line is you did something you knew was wrong. Honey, it's not your job to take care of this family. We've always trusted God to provide and He has. He will. Trish, you should have come to us first."

"But, I was . . ." Trish paused to swallow. She dropped her head further. "I was afraid you'd say no."

"And I would have. Trish, when will you learn that we only want what's best for you?" Marge dropped her knitting in her lap. "You're exhausted. Your grades are suffering. You've been snappy. And accidents happen when people are too tired."

"Mom, I've been trying my best."

"I know."

David came in and sank down on the sofa.

"What if I promise never to do anything like this again? If I swear to always come to you first? Dad? Mom? I can't handle the guilt."

Hal nodded as he brought his recliner upright. "I know, Trish. That's why God gave us Jesus. To rid us of the guilt and teach us forgiveness."

Marge made a little sound in her throat.

"I know how hard you all have been working. And I'll never be able to tell you how grateful I am—we are," Hal included Marge, smiling at her. "I wish I could say things will get better soon." He shook his head. "But I can't." He stopped to swallow and lick his lips. With one weary hand he rubbed the creases in his forehead.

Trish felt the tears stinging again. One trickled down her cheek to match the one on her father's.

The fire snapped in the fireplace. David sniffed and got up for a tissue.

Hal blinked, then sighed.

It seemed to Trish that the weight of despair crushed her father further into his chair. She took hold of his hand and raised it to her cheek, wishing and praying that her strength would help him. *Could* help him.

"We'll just have to continue to take one step at a time. You're right, Trish. Money is a big problem. We have no health insurance and the hospital bills have already wiped out most of our savings."

Trish leaped up and dashed to the closet for her jacket. "Here." She dropped the envelopes into her father's lap. "And I'm not sure how much my check will be for the races. Over a couple thousand dollars, I think. It'll help, Dad."

Hal smiled as he read the note. "My good friends." He smoothed the bills and handed Marge the note. "Trish, this should be your money, but thanks."

Marge smiled over the note, then raised her head to smile at Trish. "I hate to take your money, too." She shook her head. "But . . . well . . . thank you, Tee."

Trish felt a warm glow spreading through her midsection.

"I have thought of getting a job, myself," Marge said after rereading the note. "But I'm not really trained for anything. However, Trish, you simply *cannot* miss school to race." Her mother's tone allowed no argument. "I know you can make the best money— if you win—but school *has* to come first. The minute your grades fall, weekday racing goes."

Trish drew a deep breath. *They weren't going to make her quit riding for other farms!*

Marge continued, "We've given you a lot of freedom in the past, but now we'll want a complete report every Sunday evening. We'll sit down for a family meeting and talk about the past week and what's coming up. There will be no more half-truths; we *must* know what's going on around here."

Hal nodded. "Your mother's right. We have to be able to trust each other. And we can't afford to have anyone else sick around here. I know how important it is for me not to worry, too. We all have to believe that God knows what He's doing. He's always taken care of us in the past and now is no exception. He *will* provide, but we have to work together." He looked intently at each member of the family.

Trish felt her eyes fill again. She swallowed past

the lump in her throat and nodded.

Hal let his hands fall at his sides and resettled himself in the chair. "Now, Trish, how many mounts do you have for tomorrow?"

CHAPTER 9

Trish crawled into bed that night with her father's "I forgive you, Tee" ringing in her ears. She could also see her mother's face, the grim line about her mouth. Family meetings every week. No more fibbing about how school was going. Total honesty—or pay the consequences. She knew there would be no more stretching the boundaries. Besides, she'd learned that cheating of any kind hurt too badly. Not only herself—but her whole family.

"Thank you, heavenly Father, for bringing Dad home again. And for helping to clean up the mess I made. God, please make my Dad well again. And help me to win tomorrow. Amen." She thumped her pillow and turned over. Morning would be here before she had half enough sleep. A brief snatch of song drifted through her mind, " . . . *bear you up on eagle's wings.*" She smiled her way to dreamland.

———

Hal sat with a cup of coffee cradled in his hands at the breakfast table the next morning. His smile made Trish think the sun had broken through the heavy overcast. Her mother humming in the kitchen, bacon sizzling in the pan, David singing off-key in the shower; all seemed normal—like life was supposed to be at Runnin' On Farm.

She hugged her dad, squeezed her mom around the waist and slid into her chair. Her grin felt like it might crack her face. "Waffles!" The grin got wider. "Thanks, Mom." Crispy golden waffles were joined by two strips of bacon and an egg, easy-over, just the way she liked it. Trish buttered her waffles and poured the syrup.

"You could say grace first." Her father smiled.

Trish grinned back at him and silently bowed her head. All she could say was *Thank you, thank you, thank you.*

"See you at the track . . ." Her father hugged her before she picked up her bag and boots. David honked the horn. "In the winner's circle."

"Be careful," her mother added with a hug. Worry lines still creased her forehead.

"Sure, Mom. And thanks for the good breakfast." When Trish glanced back, Marge had leaned into the protective circle of Hal's arm. Trish suppressed the wish that her father could come along, and hung her silks behind the seat. "Let's go," she said, slamming the pickup door.

———

Trish could see the outline of the sun through the clouds as she trudged the path to the dressing room. Horses for the first race of the day were being led to the saddling paddock. Her mom and dad hadn't shown up at the track yet, but she, David and Brad had Spitfire and Gatesby in prime form. After the ruckus he'd caused the evening before, Gatesby had clowned around, tossing David's hat, dribbling water on Trish's back when she tried to pick his hooves. Trish smiled at the memory.

"You look happy." Genie Stokes caught up with her.

"I am. Dad says he'll be here today." Trish grinned at the other jockey. "How's your shoulder?"

"Stiffens up some," Genie swung her arm in an arc. "But the pain is gone. That Spitfire sure didn't like having someone else on his back."

"Sorry."

"Hey, it's not your fault. By the way, you heard what they're saying about you?"

"No. Who?"

"Oh here and there. They say either you're luckier'n anyone or you just talk those horses into winning. Not too often someone comes along with that special touch, but I think you got it."

"I . . . I just do what seems best." Trish shifted her bag to her other hand. "Are the other jockeys. . . ?"

"Well, there's some griping. You know how people can be—but most everyone is glad for you. They know about your dad and all."

Trish slowed as they reached the slanted concrete tunnel to the dressing rooms. "Thanks, Genie. You've helped me a lot."

"Just repaying the favor. You know your dad has helped plenty of people around this track. Both with advice and money when times are tough. Me included. He's a good man."

Trish felt a glow of pride. She'd always known her dad was the best. Genie's words just proved it. "Thanks."

At the whiff of dressing room, her butterflies woke up and began their warm-up routine just like the one she was about to perform. Trish had forgotten to appreciate their long nap. They'd even slept through a waffle breakfast. What a day!

Spitfire nickered when he saw Trish waiting in the saddling stall. He seemed to dance on the tips of his hooves as he followed David. Head up, ears pricked, he caught the attention of the railbirds, those watching the saddling process. At their "oohs" and "aahs," he lifted his nose higher, like a movie star with fans.

"You silly." Trish laughed as David tied the slipknot in the stall. "You think everyone came just to see you."

Spitfire nodded. He shoved his nose against her chest and snuffled her pockets. Trish held out both fists. When he licked the right one, she gave him the hidden carrot.

"I dare you to do that with Gatesby." David fastened the saddle girth.

"Sure. And lose my hand. How could I ride then?" Trish smoothed Spitfire's forelock. When he begged for another carrot, she laughed and pushed his persistent nose away. "After you win." She looked him straight in the eye. "Now give it all you've got, Spitfire. We need the money."

David boosted her into the saddle. "Watch that far turn. It seemed wet." He patted her knee. "You can do it."

"Did you see Mom and Dad?"

"They're up in the box." David backed Spitfire out and handed the lead shank to Brad mounted on Dan'l. He patted Spitfire on the rump. "Go get 'em."

As the bugle blew parade, Spitfire danced to the side of the gray. He flung his head up at the flags snapping in the breeze. When the crowd roared, he turned his head, accepting their accolades.

"Should have named you Prince or King." Trish laughed in sheer joy. "Or maybe Ham."

Brad laughed with her as he released the lead. "Ham he is. See you in the circle."

At the post position, Spitfire settled for the break. Within three lengths after the shot, he was running easily at the head of the field. No other horse even came near him. Trish felt like they were out for a private gallop. She heard the announcer call Genie Stokes as rider of the second-place finisher.

"Congratulations," Trish called as they cantered their horses back to the circle.

Genie stopped her mount. "Did he even go all out?" She pointed her whip at Spitfire.

"I don't think so. But he sure had fun." Trish smoothed Spitfire's mane. "He wasn't too happy about quitting."

"You might be thinking first Saturday in May," Genie grinned. "He's some horse, even if he doesn't like any other riders."

Trish felt a tingle go up her spine and then race down again. *The first Saturday in May. Kentucky Derby Day.* While she and her dad had dreamed about it, someone else mentioning it made the dream more of a reality.

She slipped from her horse's back and removed the saddle. Standing between her father and David with Spitfire's head over her shoulder felt right. This was where they all belonged—in the winner's circle.

"Congratulations, Tee." Her father kissed her cheek. Spitfire nudged Hal away, as if he were jealous. Laughter from the crowd, another popping flash and Trish got on the scale. She could get to like this.

Trish changed silks, weighed in again, and joined David and Gatesby for the next race. "What'd you feed these guys today?" she asked after the colt tried to pick the silk covering off her helmet. When she scolded him, the horse gave her his *who—me?* look.

"They're sure full of spunk today. Leading him over here was tougher than an hour on the weights. And that was with Brad on the other lead. All you'll have to do is point him in the right direction and hang on today."

"Thank you for making my job sound so simple." Trish thumped her brother on the head with her whip. "Is Anderson here?"

"Up in the box. He came by the stable, but says you know Gatesby better than he does. So just do your best. Dad says since you're on the outside, stay there. And he'll see you in the circle again. He said to tell you this could get to be a habit. A nice habit."

"Yep." Trish gathered her reins as David led them out. Gatesby didn't think he should wait until the end of the line. All those horses in front of him and . . .

"Knock it off, you big goof." Trish pulled him back to a walk. When he crowhopped, Brad jerked on the rope. Trish snugged the reins down until Gatesby's chin met his chest. Even then, he pranced sideways instead of walking.

"How're your arms?" David released the lead.

Trish laughed. "See ya."

"In the circle."

Gatesby walked into the gate flatfooted and settled for the break, all business now that the time was at hand. When the gates clanged open, he erupted, running flat out within four strides. Trish kept him on the outside, letting the field spread itself. Gatesby pulled on the bit, running smoothly, his concentration focused on the horses ahead of him.

As they passed the half-way pole, Trish gave him more rein. He passed the third-place runner, caught the second and reached for the first as they entered the final stretch.

"Now, go for it!" Trish commanded. "Come on, Gatesby!"

"And the winner by a nose, Number Seven, Gatesby, owned by John Anderson and ridden by Tricia Evanston." The announcer confirmed what Trish already knew. She had won again. And Gatesby had lived up to her expectations. "Good boy! You were great."

"Knock it off, you dummy," Trish hissed at the horse when John Anderson flinched. Gatesby acted as though the bruise on Anderson's shoulder had nothing to do with him. So what if he was in the winner's circle. A shoulder right next to his nose was too good a target to pass up.

Anderson rubbed the bruise as David led Gatesby away to the testing barn. "He never gives up, does he?" John turned to Hal. "Thought you could break him of that."

Hal and Trish looked at each other and shook their

heads. "We tried. At least he doesn't bite hard anymore. Just nips." Trish stepped off the scale. "He thinks he's being funny."

"Some joker. Thanks, Trish. You did a good job."

As Anderson disappeared into the crowd, Trish joined her mom and dad at the rail. Hal sank back into his wheelchair. "That's enough for one day." He looked up at his wife. "Ready to go home?"

"Sure was good to have you here." Trish walked beside him. "Even if Spitfire doesn't like that kissing stuff."

Hal chuckled. "He's your horse all right. See you at home."

———

Trish felt a letdown after the next race. She brought Bob Diego's horse in second. While the owner was pleased, Trish missed the winner's circle. But she knew she'd ridden a good race. The horse had done his best, too. The winner had just been better.

"Hey, two out of three's not bad." Brad joined her in the lawn chairs in the tackroom. He handed her a can of soda. "Drink this and let's get out of here."

———

It was hard to hit the books after such an exciting day. But when Trish thought of her bed, she remembered the discussion from the night before. Her grades *had* to stay at a B or better. The cards on the wall caught her eye. "Give thanks." "He cares for you." She picked up her pencil. *Chlorine, Cl; Chromium, Cr. . . .*

———

The next morning in church Trish chose to pay attention. The praise hymns suited her mood. Praising God wasn't so hard when her father was next to her in the pew. During the offering they all sang the new song, "He will raise you up on eagle's wings. Bear you on the breath of God." She listened hard for the words. The tune seemed planted forever in her mind. She decided to look up the verse later.

———————

Firefly won that afternoon. *Maybe this is God's way of helping us out right now. Giving us the money we need.* Her thoughts leapfrogged ahead of her feet as she walked back to the dressing room to change for the next race. *Just now we need horses that are able to win, and we have them. And I can ride, so we don't need to pay jockey fees.* She shook her head. *Amazing.*

"If you can get her in the money at all, I'll be pleased," Jason Rodgers said as he boosted Trish into the saddle for the seventh race. "There's a tough field out there."

"Well, old girl," Trish said as she stroked her mount's neck on the way back to the scale. "I know you did your best, so it's a good thing your boss will be happy with a show. Third place isn't my favorite, but . . . guess it's better than no money at all."

"Good job." Rodgers shook Trish's hand. "I have two on Wednesday's program. Both late in the day. Can you ride them?"

"I think so, but I'll let you know later this evening."

"That's fine. Sure was good to see Hal here yesterday. Tell him hello for me. He got away before I could get to him."

Trish felt that familiar pride straighten her tired shoulders. She had to remember to tell her dad what Genie had said. It was a shame he couldn't have been there to see Firefly win, but yesterday had worn him out.

Marge had dinner ready to put on the table when Trish and David walked in the door. Trish couldn't believe her eyes when she sat down. Roast beef, mashed potatoes, gravy—her mother must have spent all afternoon cooking.

"Smells wonderful!" Hal laid his napkin in his lap. After grace he raised his head and looked at Trish. "Now, tell me how the day went."

Trish talked between bites. "Mom, this is so-o-o good." She and David related all the happenings of the afternoon, and Trish finished with Genie's comments. "She said you've helped lots of people when they needed it."

"I just do what I can." Hal leaned back in his chair. "You know we've always shared what we have. And God's been good to us."

Trish looked at her father. His plaid shirt hung loosely on his once-broad shoulders. The circles under his eyes had deepened to dark hollows. Even his thin hair seemed to have grayed, matching the lines in his face. And purple and black bruises covered the back of one hand from the IV's. After all he'd been through the last couple of months, her dad could say, "God's been good to us." *Maybe he means for the past—not for now.*

"I mean it, Tee." He seemed to read her mind. "God is good to us right now—today and every day. I'm here, aren't I?"

Trish nodded. Saying thanks for winning was easy. But her father said thanks no matter what.

"Now. How many mounts have you been offered this week?"

Trish told him about the offers. "But I said I'd let them know tonight." She looked at her mother. "And while I have more studying, my chemistry is caught up. I'm okay for this week."

"So far." Marge sipped her coffee. "See if you can get to bed early tonight."

"What about the rumors you mentioned, David?" Hal pushed his chair back. "Let's go in the other room where the chairs are more comfortable."

"Diego wondered if you were considering Spitfire for the first Saturday in May. He said to call him if there was any way he could help."

Trish snuggled against the pillow she'd stuffed between her back and the stones of the hearth. "Genie asked the same thing. We've said this is our year."

"I know." Hal sighed. "I just . . . well, we have to take one step at a time. The Futurity is the next milestone. That's a mile and an eighth, close to the Derby. Spitfire needs plenty of conditioning to run that far."

Trish sizzled with excitement. "You mean we're gonna try for it?"

"God only knows, Tee. God only knows."

CHAPTER 10

"So. What all happened?" Rhonda blocked her way in the school hall.

"Well, I won."

"All right!"

"Three times."

"Three times? On who?"

"Spitfire, Gatesby, and Firefly. Got a second and a third on the other two." Trish twirled the dial on her locker. "And I have two rides for Wednesday."

"Did you tell your dad . . . about the . . ."

"Extra racing? Yes."

"And you're still alive—and still riding? Trish, for crying out loud, quit stalling and start talking."

"And start walking." Brad wrapped an arm about each of them and herded them toward the lunchroom. "I'm starved."

It took the entire lunch period to fill her friends in on all the details. Brad added a few of his own. "And so," Trish finished, "we start seriously training Spitfire for the Futurity and then we'll see about . . ."

"The first Saturday in May?" Rhonda couldn't stand still and remain cool. Brad finally put both hands on her shoulders to calm her down.

The bell rang. Rhonda hugged Trish and dashed off.

Trish had to order her mind to quit dreaming of the Derby. Her classes came first. She needed every bit of concentration she could scare up.

————

When she got home, Trish found her father in the recliner reading his Bible. He put it down when she entered the living room. "Come sit here a minute," he patted the hearth in front of the snapping fire.

"Wait a sec." Trish raised her book bag. In the bedroom she dropped her load beside the cluttered desk. Her room seemed to grow piles of clothes when she wasn't looking. She shut her eyes on the mess and went back to her dad by way of the kitchen for milk and an apple.

"How was your day, Trish?"

"Good." She offered him a bite of her apple. "Finals are this week, so the teachers kind of let up today."

"I've been thinking about the logistics around here. You need to get your driver's license so people don't have to keep hauling you around."

"All right!" Trish's grin nearly cracked her jaw.

"Do you have time to take the test soon?"

"Well, my chemistry final on Thursday is my last hard one. I only have history on Friday, so Thursday afternoon would work. We have Anderson's horse running on Friday and I have one other mount."

"Fine. Your mother will pick you up at school on Thursday afternoon, then." Hal returned her grin. "Just make sure you pass the first time."

"Da-a-d." She drained her glass of milk. "Gotta go work those beasts. You been down to see Miss Tee yet? She's really growing."

Hal shook his head. "I'll be down to watch tomorrow afternoon."

Trish spent the week studying. Every spare minute she reviewed Spanish vocabulary, chemistry symbols, and Shakespeare for English. Her two mounts on Wednesday finished in the money but not the winner's circle. While she was disappointed, Bob Diego congratulated her for good rides. He offered her two more on Saturday and one on Sunday.

"Sorry you can't ride during the day," he said. "I'd like you up on Friday afternoon."

"Me too."

Another trainer asked Trish to ride on Saturday.

I'm going to have to keep a calendar, Trish thought on the way home. *In fact, I need to be better organized. Somehow, I've got to keep my room clean. That'd make Mom happier than anything . . . other than quitting my racing, that is.*

Trish was up till 3:00 A.M. on Thursday. Even though David coached her in the evening, she felt she hadn't done enough. All the equations and symbols ran together—mixed with racing times, and at how many feet one must dim the car lights for an oncoming vehicle.

Trish slept right through her alarm. When she finally heard the insistent buzzer, the clock read 7:10.

"Trish, you're going to be late."

"I'm up."

"That's what you said 15 minutes ago." Marge wiped her hands on a dish towel as she leaned against the door frame.

"I did?" Trish shook her head and tried to blink her eyes open. "I don't remember."

"How can you stand . . ." Marge cut off her words, but Trish knew what she wanted to say. One glance at her mother's face after seeing her totalled room said it all.

Not today. Not this week. Trish stumbled down the hall to the shower. *Maybe I'll have time to clean it up Saturday.*

The hot shower helped wake her up but her eyes still felt gritty, as if she had to force her eyelids to stay open.

"Control to Trish, come in Trish." David teased her in the car.

"Umm-mmm," Trish yawned for the umpteenth time. "I should go out and run the track." She picked up her book bag. "I just can't wake up."

"I noticed."

She felt good about her Spanish test. The essay went well, too. But she felt totally defeated by the chemistry test. *Why can't I get this stuff?* Tears of frustration pricked the backs of her eyelids. *I've never studied so hard for anything in my life.* She slumped into her seat in history class. The hour was slated for review, with the teacher answering questions and approving topics for term papers next quarter. Trish opened her book. Panic swept over her. She hadn't even thought of a topic yet.

Half an hour later the teacher shook her awake.

"I'll have to call your parents right after school," she warned. "You're just too tired, Trish. Something has to give."

Trish just shook her head and muttered as she left the room. She felt like slamming her fist into her locker door when it wouldn't open. A perfect end to a perfect day? Right!

Trish waved at Rhonda and Brad, then tossed her book bag in the back seat of the family car.

"Feel like driving?" Marge opened the door and stepped out.

"I guess so."

"Pretty bad day, huh?"

Trish just nodded as she slid into the driver's seat. The nagger added to her weariness. *You better tell her. You know you promised.* Trish felt like twisting his scrawny neck, if he had such a thing. *I planned on it,* she answered. *Give me a break, will ya?* She bit her lip. That wasn't quite true. She *had* thought about postponing telling her mother.

As they turned on to 79th Street, heading west to Hazel Dell, Trish glanced over at her mother. Marge sat half-turned in the seat, studying her daughter.

"I did fine in Spanish and English, maybe flunked chemistry, and fell asleep in history." Trish got it all out in a rush. "Mrs. Smith will call you to set up a conference. She's probably trying to get you now."

"Oh, Trish." Marge patted her daughter's arm. "I'm sorry."

Yeah, I'll bet. The words popped into Trish's mind. Then she scolded herself. It wasn't as if her mother didn't care.

"I tried *so* hard." She ground her teeth together. "And it didn't do any good."

"When will you know your grades?"

"Tomorrow."

Marge nodded. "Are you sure you feel up to your driving test today?"

"Yeah." Trish took a deep breath. "Mom, I *have* to ride tomorrow. I gave my word."

"I know. But remember the agreement, nothing below a B. You can ride tomorrow because the grades aren't posted yet, but don't accept anything beyond that—until you know."

Trish groaned.

"And falling asleep in class . . ." Marge straightened in her seat, took a deep breath, and shook her head. "Your father and I will talk with Mrs. Smith." She looked at Trish slumped behind the wheel. "How about something to eat before you go in there?"

"Afterwards, okay? I just want to get this over with."

Trish didn't need to tell her mother she'd passed the written driver's test. Her grin said it all when she emerged from the room. "My behind-the-wheel appointment is next Tuesday." She slid into the driver's seat. "I can't believe I got one so soon. They had a cancellation." She reread her score sheet. "I missed the questions on numbers again—four of them. They all had to do with number of feet and speeds. I *hate* numbers." She stuffed the sheet into her purse. "Let's go eat."

———

"Mrs. Smith called," Marge said when Trish came back to the house after working the horses that night. "Our conference is for Monday right after school"

"Me too?"

Marge nodded. "Dinner's ready."

Trish started to get ready for bed early that night, resenting the hour she'd spent on history. She felt that if she didn't do well on that final, it would be another strike against her in Mrs. Smith's eyes. She glared at her notes.

Reaching to turn out the light, she stared at the open book on her desk. With a groan she threw back the covers, stomped to the desk, and grabbed the book. Propping her pillow against the headboard, she began reviewing—again. She *would* get an A on this one.

————

Or close to it. When she'd finished the test, only two true and false questions were in doubt, and the written part looked good. At the end of the day Trish slammed her locker, and she and Rhonda dashed to the parking lot. Even a mud bath from a sloppy track would be better than the last couple of days. But then, anything to do with horses was better than finals.

"What'd you get in chemistry?" Rhonda leaned on the back of the front seat.

"C–. One point away from a D." Trish slumped in the seat. "At least they won't ground me today. But I'll have to tell Diego I can't ride Wednesday."

"Maybe your mom and dad will change their minds."

"No." Trish shook her head. "No chance. And

they're meeting with Mrs. Smith on Monday. I'll probably have to quit racing on weekdays all together."

"It's just not fair."

"Tell me about it."

"Your dad coming to watch?" Brad asked.

"I don't think so. David's already there to get Final Command ready. My first mount is for Diego."

———

Trish rode to win the fourth race. While the pouring rain washed half the mud off her black and white silks, her grin still sparkled. Wet or dry, she loved the winner's circle.

Final Command fidgeted in the gate. "That's not like you, fella," Trish crooned as she stroked his neck. "I know you don't like the rain, so let's just get this over with."

The horse on their right refused to enter the starting stall. It took two assistants to finally get him in. Trish hunched her shoulders to keep the rain from running down her neck. She crouched forward, making herself small, hugging all her body heat close. Mentally she called the stubborn horse every name she could think of.

"If only we were on the outside, boy." She spoke to her mount's twitching ears. "But we're right in the middle."

And in the middle was where they were six lengths out of the gate. Right in the middle with horses slipping all around them. She felt a bump on one side and pulled back on the reins to get them out of the melee before something happened.

At that moment, she heard the crack of a bat. Her mount leaped forward. They slammed into the horse on their left.

Someone had struck her horse!

CHAPTER 11

Pure strength of will kept her horse on its feet. Trish ignored the stumbling animals around them and kept her mount's head up. He slipped in the mud but regained his footing. As the way cleared ahead of them, Trish talked him into running the race. Far ahead the two leaders rounded the turn. One other horse left the pack and ran with her.

Trish brought the animal over to the rail and as she encouraged him with heart, hands and voice, they ate up the furlongs. While there was no way to catch the lead runners, she made sure that they took third place. As they raced around the track, her mind returned to the thwap of a bat on *her* mount's haunches.

"I'm sorry that someone hit you, fella. I know you're not used to the whip. You don't need it. But who hit you? And why?"

That was her question to her father that evening. "Why, Dad? Why would someone hit my horse? And who? Who would do such a mean thing? It's illegal, too, isn't it?"

"Did you report it?"

"No. I don't know how. And it was such a mess out there, I . . . I just wanted to get home." She leaned even closer to the roaring fire. She wasn't sure she would ever feel warm again. On the outside anyway. Inside she was hotter than the snapping logs.

"It's just so unfair!" Sparks from the fire reflected in her eyes.

"Trish, life isn't fair. Racing isn't fair. There will always be those who do underhanded things. Those who take advantage of others. Even to the point of cruelty. That's part of racing. Part of any business."

"And that's why I'd rather you weren't racing." Marge stepped into the room, handing her daughter a steaming cup of hot chocolate.

"But, M-o-m."

"One of the horses went down, and it could easily have been you." She raised her hand to stop Trish's answer.

"I know you're a good rider. And I thank God you weren't injured, that no one was seriously hurt. But accidents happen. And maliciousness. You felt it first-hand." She turned back to the kitchen. "Dinner'll be ready in about fifteen minutes. Set the table, please, Trish, as soon as you finish your chocolate."

Trish cupped the hot mug in her hands.

"She's right, you know," her dad said.

"I know, but . . ."

"Tomorrow we'll file a complaint, so you know how."

"That's not all." Trish swirled the remaining cocoa in her mug. "I got a C– on my chemistry test."

"I'm sorry, Tee."

Not half as sorry as I am, Trish thought as she got up to set the table. *I'm the one who has to tell those men I can't ride. And that's gonna shoot down my pay-check for next week.*

Trish enjoyed picking up her check each week from the head office at the track. Giving the money to her father made her feel like all the hours she put in made a difference for their family. No matter how much her father grumbled about her not keeping the money, she knew the bills were being paid. And that made his life easier.

"I want to make Dad's life easier, so he can get well, Father," she prayed that night. "Thank you for the money, and for keeping me safe." She snuggled down in the covers. "And please help me find out who whipped us today. Amen."

When Trish came up from working the horses in the morning, her mother had scrambled eggs with bacon ready to put on the table. She pulled a pan of bran muffins from the oven as Trish slid into her place.

"Those guys were sure rarin' to go this morning," Trish rubbed her arms. "I feel like I did a hundred push-ups."

"How would you know?" David asked. "You've never done that many at one time." He put his plateful of food down on the table. "Thanks, Mom. This smells great."

Trish stuck her tongue out at him. "Well, you work four horses and see how your arms feel."

Hal buttered a muffin. "What time do you have to be at the track?"

"One or so. I ride in the third and fifth."

"Good. David, I want you to bring all the horses home today. I know that's not the best, but it will be easier for you to have them all here. Plus we won't have to pay the extra help at the track."

David nodded.

"And Tee, how about showing off that little filly of yours right after breakfast?"

"Um-m-m," Trish scrunched up her face. "I've got something I have to do first."

Surprise raised her father's eyebrows. "Okay. Let me know when you're ready."

———

Trish attacked her room with a vengeance. Some clothes ended up on hangers for the first time in days while others landed in the washing machine. The jumbled bed took on a completely new look when the bedspread was smoothed into place. And her desk—there really was a flat surface under all those papers.

An hour later she folded her underwear and stacked it in the proper drawer. A quick swipe with the dustcloth and even the chest of drawers shone. "God, help me keep this up," she prayed as she looked around the orderly room. "Even I can't stand the mess anymore, let alone Mom." She gathered a pile of shirts off the chair and headed for the laundry room. "I'm ready." She turned the dial to start the last wash load.

———

Miss Tee still spooked when someone else tried to approach her but she came right up to Trish. The bright morning sun made her blink as Trish led the mare out of the barn and turned her loose in the paddock. When the mare snorted and rolled in the wet grass, the filly danced over to Trish, and hiding on the opposite side from Hal, rubbed her forehead against Trish's arm. When she peeked around to keep that strange man in sight, Trish chuckled. Hal coughed. Miss Tee darted away, her hooves skimming the grass. She skidded to a stop behind the standing mare, then peeked out, her nose and ears visible through her mother's tail.

"She's a beauty, all right." Hal leaned against the fence, resting his elbows on the board rail. "But she should be with her bloodlines. Full sister to Spitfire. Only shame is her birthday. She'll be barely three months old January 1st."

"Yeah, but legally she'll be a year. It's crazy that all thoroughbreds are considered a year old on January 1st, no matter when they were dropped." The filly tiptoed back to Trish. She reached around, tentatively sniffed Hal's arm and shook her head.

Hal laughed. "Come on, Tee. We've got work to do."

Just for a moment, if she didn't look at her father, Trish could pretend things were just as they used to be. But then he coughed again. He turned toward the house, his once-broad shoulders hunched against the chill of the morning, and his face slashed with new lines and gray like the fog.

But at least he's down here with you and not in the hospital, her nagger reminded. *Don't you ever take a nap?* Trish snapped back, but then smiled at herself. She knew she needed to remember to be thankful.

That afternoon she won both races. Both owners seemed as pleased as she was. The best part was that her father had watched from the special bleachers built by the barns for owners and trainers to observe morning workouts.

Trish could feel her Irish temper flare when he told her what he'd heard. The jockey, whose horse went down the day before, had filed a complaint against Trish for knocking him down.

"You can't prove someone struck you," Hal said when Trish fumed. "I told them what happened, but . . ."

"No good." Trish drew circles in the shavings with her booted toe. She chewed on her bottom lip. "At least my side is written down too, right?"

Hal nodded.

Trish was silent as they loaded Firefly and Dan'l. She checked Final Command's legs before leading him into the trailer. At least he hadn't been hurt in the accident.

But it wasn't an accident. She climbed into the truck cab beside her dad. *We were slashed on purpose.*

The organ was playing her song when they entered the church sanctuary the next morning. Trish hummed along. Eagle's wings. She sure needed them. She glanced at her father. So did he.

After church she took her Bible and checked the concordance. Isaiah 40:31. She looked up the verse and wrote it down—twice—on two cards. "But they that wait for the Lord shall renew their strength, they shall mount up with wings like eagles, they shall run and not be weary, they shall walk and not faint."

Her father was sound asleep in his recliner. Trish slipped the card into the Bible lying on the end table by his chair. Picking up the quilt, she covered him gently. *Wish you could come along, Dad. I need you there. And get better, I need you here.* She felt the plea so powerfully, she was afraid she'd spoken out loud. Then Trish changed clothes and left for the track. She had three mounts ahead.

A stiff breeze had the flags on the infield snapping. That same western breeze trailed mare's tails across the washed-out blue sky. While bringing in more wet weather, it had also helped dry the track.

Trish took time with her first mount. She hadn't ridden the mare before, but Rodgers had assured her the horse had every chance of being in the money. Still, she was a long shot on the boards.

"Well, old girl, let's go for the top. You'll look good in those pictures." Trish gathered her reins and settled her goggles in place. She needed a win as bad as the horse. Thoughts of the whip from the day before flitted into her mind as the gates closed, but she shut them out and concentrated on her mount.

That concentration paid off—handsomely. The purse was a large one. But Jason Rodgers still handed her an envelope. "I can't believe it," he said after the pictures were taken. "You brought her in two lengths ahead of the favorite."

"She just wanted to run," Trish laughed with him. "And I let her. Thanks for . . . for . . ." she touched her pocket.

Rodgers nodded. "Tell your dad hello for me."

By the end of the sixth race, Trish was jubilant. Two wins, a second and no whip. Surely yesterday had been a freak.

Her good humor lasted until the family meeting that evening. Even though her mind knew she would be grounded for her chemistry grade, her heart kept hoping her parents would change their minds. They didn't.

If I hear 'It's for your own good' one more time—I— I. To not race was *not* for her own good, she was sure, and it *would* hurt the entire family. They needed her share of the purses.

Calling Jason Rodgers and Bob Diego were two of the hardest things she'd ever had to do. "I'm sorry, I can't ride for you during the week," she said. To answer their "whys" she was tempted to blame her parents, but honesty won over. "I let my grades go down, but I can still ride Saturdays and Sundays." She felt like slamming the receiver down, but instead grabbed her jacket and slammed out the door.

Caesar shoved his cold nose into her hand, but after no response, trotted beside her down to the dark stables.

"It's just not fair," she sobbed into Dan'l's mane.

"I'm trying my best and it just isn't good enough. It's not fair."

An hour later, all cried out, she slipped back into the house and crawled into bed. "God, you said you would help me. Where are you?"

———————

"It happened, didn't it." Rhonda didn't need more than one look at Trish's face to know. "Until when?"

"My grade comes back up. And today we have the conference with Mrs. Smith." Trish leaned against her locker. "You'd think all my good grades would count for something, but no. One crummy . . . I hate chemistry!"

Trish felt like she was invisible as Mrs. Smith and her parents discussed her grades, her exhaustion, her future grades, and what she planned to do with her life. Nobody asked her.

She swallowed a smart remark. When she shifted in her chair for the third time, her father turned his head and winked at her. A warm glow, like a hug, circled her heart.

She caught herself just before a yawn. That's all she needed. To fall asleep during the conference.

"So, we'll set up a conference with our counselor, Mrs. Olson, the principal, and Trish's other teachers, if that's all right?" Mrs. Smith asked.

Trish jerked completely alert. *Now what?*

At her parents' nod, she continued. "Would tomorrow be possible?"

"No." Hal shook his head. "I have another treatment tomorrow. I won't be in any shape for a meeting. How about Thursday?"

Trish cleared her throat. "Will you need me there?"

The three nodded.

"I'll call you then," Mrs. Smith finished. "Thank you for coming."

———

The next afternoon Marge picked Trish up after school.

"How's Dad?" Trish asked as she slid behind the wheel.

"Sleeping. The doctor gave him a new medication for the nausea, so he shouldn't be so sick this time. He's gained a couple of pounds—that was good news."

Trish tried to concentrate on her driving. Surely the driver's test wasn't much different than a horse race. Her butterflies didn't need to try anything new. The old antics stirred her up enough.

"You can do it." Marge smiled through the open window after she'd slid out of the car.

The uniformed instructor who took her place looked as if a smile might shatter his face. *Maybe the frozen look is in for testing instructors.* Trish swallowed . . . hard. Her left hand refused to leave the wheel when the man told her to test the turn signals. At his second gruff order, her hand finally obeyed.

Trish relaxed as the driving got under way. She followed each instruction, but every time the man wrote something down, her butterflies did flips.

"You did just fine," he said when she parked the car back at the station. He handed her the sheet. A big red 90 stood out at the top. "Now go inside to line B to have your picture taken, and pay your fee." He almost smiled. But not quite.

Trish didn't know if her feet were touching the ground or not. When she got back in the car, her grin told her success.

"Congratulations, Trish. I'm proud of you." Marge reached across the seat to hug her daughter. "How about a banana split to celebrate?"

"You're on!" She bounced on the seat and thumped the steering wheel. *I should run around the block. I am s-o-o excited*. Instead, she carefully checked both ways before pulling out on the street.

———

As soon as they arrived home, Trish called Rhonda. "You are talking to a *licensed* driver," she said with a haughty note. Rhonda's squeal matched the one stuck about mid-throat for Trish. "Gotta run," she cut the conversation short. "Have to work the beasts."

Her dad wasn't in his recliner, but lay curled on his side in bed, asleep. The pan on the floor reminded Trish of how sick he could be. She tiptoed out without sharing her good news. This was life—since the cancer. Her dad wasn't there to share her news, good or bad.

CHAPTER 12

The weight bearing Trish down seemed even heavier on Wednesday. She hadn't been able to concentrate the night before, so instead of acing her chemistry quiz, she flunked it. Even though the sun played hide-and-seek with the scurrying clouds, she saw only gray. And rain.

Dumping her book bag on the chair at her desk, she looked around her bedroom. It seemed strange to see uncluttered carpet, undraped chairs and a *made* bed. At least *one* thing in her life was going right. Not training horses in the morning gave her the extra few minutes to put things away. *Yeah, sure,* she responded to her nagger. *Be thankful for small favors.*

Downstairs, her father asked from his seemingly permanent place in the recliner, "You got a minute, Tee?"

"Yeah," Trish answered on her way to the kitchen. "Umm-mmm, smells good." She sniffed the glorious aroma. "Wow, homemade rolls!"

Marge had just lifted the pan from a plate of caramel-cinnamon rolls. Trish scooped a golden glob of the gooey concoction from the waxed paper. "Whoa! That's hot!"

Marge turned from the sink. "Pour some milk, and I'll fix a plate of these for you and your dad. This should tempt his appetite."

"Does mine. Where's David?"

"Down at the barn, where else? He's trying to get some training in for the yearlings. We think we have a buyer for one or two of them."

Trish caught her glass before it cracked on the counter. *Selling the yearlings! Those are our investment for next year.* She swallowed the words before they could burst forth. Setting the glasses of milk and plate of rolls on a tray, she carried them into the living room.

"I know, Tee." Hal had heard and knew she was upset. "But I don't know what else to do."

"You could let me race more!"

Hal closed his eyes. He shook his head. "I know, but . . ."

"Don't say it."

A tiny smile lifted the lines around his mouth. "All right, I won't, but even if you're racing four days a week, you can't always count on a win. We can't depend completely on what you make."

"There's the money from Anderson."

"I know. That helps with the feed bill." He took a bite of the cinnamon roll. "Ah, now this is good. Your mother sure knows how to bake."

Trish huddled on the hearth. Today, even the glowing fire didn't warm the chill of foreboding that seeped into her mind like fog tendrils in the pasture hollows when the sun goes down.

"Trish, you can't carry the weight for all of us." He

pulled her card out of his Bible. "Eagle's wings," he mused. "I've loved this verse for so many years. And when the pain's been at its worst, this promise lifts me up. God does what He promises, Tee. He gives us new strength for each day, but He won't take care of tomorrow until it comes. And we can't either."

Trish nodded. "I guess so."

"I don't just guess, I *know*." Hal patted her hand. "Now, eat your roll before it's cold." He wiped his mouth. "And thanks for the card. Finding this promise has meant the world to me."

Trish sighed. She wrapped her arms around her legs and rested her chin on her knees. "It just seems crazy to keep me from racing when we need the money so badly."

"We need *you* more."

The phone rang. After a few minutes, Marge leaned around the door to the kitchen. "That was Mrs. Olson. Our meeting is being postponed until next Thursday."

Trish wasn't sure if she was happy or sad about the change. "After all, I don't even know what the meeting is really about," she confided to Caesar as he loped beside her to the stables. A sharp bark assured her that he was listening. "I sure don't need anyone yakking about my grades again, or making a big deal of my falling asleep in class."

———

"Hey, can you sleep over tomorrow night?" Trish asked Rhonda on the way to the cafeteria the next morning. "We're trailering Firefly and Gatesby to the track right after school, then I need to gallop Spitfire and you could ride Final Command. I already asked my mom."

"Don't know why not. I'll ask and call you tonight."

"Maybe we could rent a movie."

"What about me?" Brad thumped his hand on his chest. "All I do is work all the time. I *never* get invited to the parties."

Trish and Rhonda rolled their eyes at each other. "You can bring the soft drinks."

The horses loaded without a hitch. After David and Brad rolled out of the driveway, Trish and Rhonda galloped the two at home, fed all the stock, and still had time to play with Miss Tee.

Only twinges of I-wish-I-were-at-the-track nipped at Trish's mind. If she were forced to admit it, the break felt good.

And the party felt better. For a party it was, as Hal teased Rhonda about her latest boyfriend, and *everyone* hassled Trish about *the* Doug Ramstead. Marge served hamburgers and French fries, with ice cream sundaes for dessert. By the time they brought in the popcorn, Trish felt as if she might pop.

Halfway through the movie, Rhonda had an attack of the giggles. Her face turned red and tears streamed down her face.

"It must be a v-v-virus," Trish tried to talk around her own laughter.

"Knock it off, you two," David threw a pillow at Rhonda.

"We can't hear the movie!" Brad raised his hands in protest.

Trish was rolling on the floor. Rhonda thumped her

feet. Neither of them could breathe.

"Don't look at me!" Trish plumped the pillow on Rhonda's head. "Or I'll never stop." Their laughter erupted again.

Trish took a deep breath. When she looked up at her dad, he winked at her. She lay on her back, staring up at the pine-board ceiling. Her stomach hurt from all the laughter. What a good feeling!

———

Later in her bedroom, Trish leaned over the side of her bed. Rhonda lay snug in a sleeping bag spread on foam cushions, her head propped on her hand. "We haven't gone crazy like *that* in a long time."

Trish shook her head. "Too long."

They talked for a while longer, until Rhonda didn't answer. Trish was too sleepy to prod her.

———

The next afternoon, Trish rode two races before Gatesby—winning one and placing fourth in the other. Just the thought of having her dad in the stands sent an extra thrill down her spine as she and Gatesby paraded to the post. The rain had stopped, but the track was still wet. A brisk wind bit through her silks and snapped the infield flags.

Gatesby wanted to run. He'd already worked up a lather before Brad turned them loose at the gates. Trish laughed at the bay's antics as the gate squeaked shut behind them. Gatesby spooked at the sound, then settled for the break. In a split-second Trish noted who rode on either side of her. Genie grinned back on the left.

Gatesby pulled ahead by the quarter pole and stayed there. After the finish line Trish had to fight him back to a trot. He shook his head at her command and sent gobs of lather to decorate her silks. She scraped a glob off her cheek as she slid to the ground in the winner's circle and wiped her hand on the colt's nose. "Looks better on you," she said, and held his bridle tightly under his chin. John Anderson gripped the other side the same way. Neither of them wanted a new bruise.

When the announcer called Firefly's race, Trish gladly slipped into her crimson and gold. She didn't get to wear their own silks half as much as she'd like. She smoothed the sleeve and snapped the colors on her helmet. Another win would sure feel great. She raised her shoulders up to her ears and relaxed them to get the kinks out.

By the time they paraded to the post, the drizzle had returned. Trish hunched her shoulders again, this time against the dampness. When they entered the starting gate, the drizzle deepened to a downpour. Firefly shook her head and laid back her ears.

"I don't like it anymore than you do." Trish rubbed the filly's neck. "So let's just get this over with." Firefly paused an instant after the gates clanged open, then leaped forward. Within six strides they were boxed in. Just the spot Trish hated and feared. A horse behind them kept her from pulling back.

She could hear her father's advice in her ears. *Just ride it out and watch for a hole.* Firefly skidded a bit in the turn. The harsh thwap of the whip and the squeal of pain sounded at the same instant.

Firefly leaped ahead, thudded into the horse on their right and clipped the hind feet of the mount in front of them. Trish fought to keep the filly's head up as horses grunted and stumbled around them. Jockeys swore, horses squealed. Seeing daylight in front, Trish drove for the opening and by sheer willpower kept her mount moving and upright.

Feeling Firefly loosen up and lengthen her stride, Trish checked the track ahead. One horse rounded the far turn. "Let's go for it, girl," she shouted. She ached to look back and see if anyone was injured. That had been too close. Who had struck Firefly? And why?

They pounded into the stretch, gaining on the leader. Rain drove in Trish's face. The horse ahead appeared and disappeared in the sheets of silvery, icy rain. Suddenly the first-place runner stumbled, almost went down, then limped along the rail in obvious pain.

Trish pulled Firefly up on the far side of the wire. They'd won—but at what cost to the other entries?

Hal wrapped a jacket around his daughter as she slid off her horse. The pictures were taken with an umbrella over the owners and cameraman.

"What happened?" her father asked as she stepped off the scale. David led Firefly away to the testing barn.

"Someone hit us! Dad, what's going on? What about the rest of the pack? And what happened to the lead horse?"

"I haven't heard. All I could think about was you."

"I'm okay. But someone caused all that. It was no accident."

Wouldn't you know, mother would be here to see this one, Trish thought as she stepped into the hot shower back in the dressing room. She wasn't sure if the shakes were caused by the cold or left over from the race. Anger, fierce and unrelenting, burned her from the inside as the water pounded her skin. Someone had whipped her horse, and maybe caused the injuries of other horses and riders. What sort of person would do such a thing? Poor Firefly. She'd never been struck with a whip in her entire life—until today. Trish ground her teeth. The filly's squeal of pain echoed in her ears.

Trish and her father filed their complaint before they left the track. Trish was still so angry, she could hardly give the correct information.

"They acted like it was *my* fault!" Trish railed on her father as they left the office.

"Easy, Trish. They'll look in to it. The rain made it difficult for anyone from the stands to see what was happening. At least no one was hurt. Let's be thankful for that."

"Except that horse broke a leg."

"Yes, but that had nothing to do with your situation. Sometimes bones just crack. It's one of the hazards of racing thoroughbreds." Hal snapped open the umbrella as they reached the exit. "Let's get back and check on Firefly."

The filly nickered at the sight of Trish. "I'm going to find out who did this," Trish muttered as she rubbed down the horse's neck and behind her ears. "I promise."

CHAPTER 13

"A complaint against *me*? Again?"

"I know. But your horse bumped the others. No one saw anyone strike Firefly. The rain made everyone extra cautious and visibility was nil."

"But, Dad, that's not fair!" Trish could feel herself losing control. She wanted to scream and pound someone—the someone who caused this. Twice now. Someone had struck her horses twice. "What are they saying?"

"That you're young and inexperienced." He dropped his voice. "And you'll do anything to win."

Trish stepped back as if struck. "But . . . but that's not true!"

"I know. I think someone is starting rumors too. Those who know us won't believe it, but others? Well, you know how it goes."

Trish stared at her father, her eyes wide with shock. She licked her dry lips and tightened her jaw. "What are they going to do about it?"

"Continue investigating."

Trish replayed the race in her mind—moment by moment. Nothing. All she could remember was disgust at being boxed in, and trying to keep Firefly on her feet. The reel played as she worked the horses around the home track; when she took a shower; and in a nightmare that left her shaking.

———

On Tuesday morning Trish found a new card. "I can do all things through him who strengthens me." Philippians 4:13. *I suppose that means not wanting to beat up whoever is doing this.*

Her nagger seemed to congratulate her, *You're right!*

And I can study in spite of everything? she asked.

Right on.

Even Chemistry?

You got it.

Trish smoothed the covers on her bed, and read the card again. She pinned it above the others. There was quite a list of promises. Now, to hang on to all of them.

———

A trailer truck drove out of the yard when Brad dropped her off after school that afternoon.

"Who was that?" she asked.

Hal studied his hands. "He bought Samba and the gray filly."

"You mean they're gone? Already?"

Hal nodded. "He met my price, Tee. Those two yearlings just bought us some breathing room."

Tears prickled at the back of Trish's eyes. She swallowed. "But I didn't even get to say goodbye."

"I know." Hal put his arm around her shoulders. "I know."

———————

That evening Trish had to turn down another mount when a trainer called her. His "Thanks, anyway," when she told him she'd be glad to ride for him on the weekend didn't help.

And now I'm supposed to study chemistry. Trish slammed the book shut. Standing up suddenly sent her chair crashing to the floor. She stomped to the window and jammed her hands in her back pockets.

Fog drifted past the mercury yardlight, creating a shimmering, circular glow. Rocks glistened in the driveway. Moisture beads on the car roof sparkled in the soft light. Trish sighed and returned to her desk. *Where were her eagle's wings tonight?*

The new card caught her eye. She gritted her teeth and opened the book again. "Please, God. It says *all things.*"

———————

The next afternoon Trish got a B on the chemistry quiz. *Well, that means a D-average for this quarter.* She felt like putting her head down and bawling. *When will I ever get to race again?*

Trish met her parents by the trophy case near the main doors. "Mrs. Olson asked me to take you to the conference room. She said the others would be there in a few minutes."

Trish pulled out a chair by her father. "I don't know what good this is gonna do," she muttered under her breath.

"Trust us." Her father patted her knee.

Trish nodded and smiled as all her teachers, the principal, and Mrs. Olson, her counselor, took their places. After general greetings and exchanges, a hush fell on the room. Trish squirmed in her seat. *I'd rather be home working the horses. At least that might do someone some good.*

Her father cleared his throat. "I think you all are somewhat aware of our situation. I have cancer, and . . ."

Trish forced herself to straighten up in her chair. The expression she wore masked the thoughts that whizzed through her brain. *Why does he have to tell everybody what's happening in our family? This is our business.*

But maybe they can help, her nagger offered.

Sure. She pulled herself back to the meeting.

"And so, I'm hoping you may have some suggestions of ways we can make life—and school—easier for our daughter."

The group nodded and spoke among themselves.

"Let me offer some ideas." Mrs. Olson smiled at Trish and her parents. She outlined several things they could do, including tutoring, summer school, and planning ahead for the times when Trish would be absent because of family matters.

"What do you suggest?" Marge asked the counselor.

"I suggest we take Trish out of chemistry," Mrs. Olson continued. "She can drop up to four credits without damaging her GPA. She's a good student." The other teachers nodded. "And I think we should do all we can to help her succeed. None of you," she smiled at Marge and Hal, "need any extra pressure right now. Trish can make up chemistry this summer at Clark College or choose to take another science. This will give her another study hall until next semester. That should cut her homework even more."

Trish couldn't believe her ears. *Drop chemistry! Wow!* She looked at each person around the table. They were all nodding and smiling. Trish peeked at her parents. Her mother wasn't smiling, but looked relieved.

Relief didn't begin to describe Trish's feelings. She felt like a helium balloon, let go. Yes, bumping on the ceiling might be a close description. This was almost as good as the winner's circle.

———

That evening, Trish took time to play with Miss Tee when she brought the mare and foal back into the barn. They spent their days out in the paddock now.

"I don't have to do chemistry tonight," she sang to the filly while brushing the mare. "All my homework is done." She hugged the inquisitive filly and kissed Miss Tee's soft nose. Trish got a lick on the cheek in return. Soft, tiny lips nibbled her hair. She cupped both hands on the filly's cheeks, and rubbed noses. "Oh, you sweety. I love you so much."

"It's good to see you so happy." Trish looked up, surprised to see her mother. Miss Tee retreated behind the mare's haunches. Then braver, she inched her way over to Trish, and peeked around her mistress.

"Isn't she beautiful?" Trish laid her arm around the foal's neck.

"Yes, she is. Dinner's ready."

"Okay." Trish rubbed her baby's ears one more time and slipped out of the stall. When she leaned back across the half-door, the filly nickered, a soft little sound that barely moved her nostrils. "Keep that up and I'll never leave." Trish stroked her one more time. "Remember, you're a winner." She turned off the lights, and together she and her mother left the barn.

"I'm really proud of you, you know," Marge said.

"Why, Mom?"

"Oh, lots of things. Your efforts in chemistry, all the hard work you do with the horses . . . keeping your room so neat and clean now."

"Thanks. I like my room better now, too. I've been praying to be better organized. Mom, I feel free tonight. Like a two-ton weight has been lifted off me. No more chemistry!"

"It was that bad, huh?"

"Yeah."

Matching strides, an arm around each other, they topped the rise to the warmly lit house.

———————

"Tonight, when Spitfire breezed that half mile, he didn't even look winded at the end." Hal leaned against the counter as Trish loaded the dishwasher.

"He wasn't. He's ready for the mile and a sixteenth, easily. Probably could do the mile and a quarter." Trish placed the last dish in the rack and shut the door.

"Well, Saturday will tell. How many mounts do you have this weekend?"

"Only four, so far. And Spitfire." Trish wiped off the counter. "Have you heard any more about the race last Sunday?"

"No, thought I'd check into it tomorrow." The two of them walked into the living room. "You worried?"

"A little." Trish crossed her legs and sank to the floor beside the recliner. "Aren't you?"

"Well if *you're* not worried, you should be," Marge joined the conversation. "Otherwise, I've got it covered."

Trish smiled. It was good to hear her mother joke about being worried. There hadn't been much joking in the family lately—not for the last few months.

"Just think—the Futurity's only a week and two days away. When he wins that one . . ." *First Saturday in May. Clear across the country to the Kentucky Derby!*

"Take one race at a time, Tee." Her father stroked her hair. "One day at a time."

———

Just before she fell asleep that night, Trish heard her father's voice, *One race at a time.* Did that mean he wasn't planning on the Derby anymore?

She'd already said her prayers, but she quickly added another. *Please God, the Derby.*

———

Even though it rained all day Friday, Trish still felt like the helium balloon. Lighter than air, she drifted through her classes—especially the extra study hall.

She used it to begin research for her history term paper.

Even though Gatesby did his best to spoil her good mood, Trish laughed at his bad humor . . . and stayed away from his teeth. A good hard workout took the starch out of him and made Trish feel even better.

Only when she galloped Firefly did the nagging worry creep back in. What if Spitfire was slashed tomorrow? So far, neither she nor her horse had been hurt, but what if their luck was running out?

She remembered what her father had said so many times. *For us, luck doesn't count. Only God counts. And His care.* "Well I sure hope He's got lots of guardian angels around us tomorrow. If I could just get my hands on whoever . . ."

———

Trish awoke suddenly from another nightmare. She breathed deeply and wiggled her fingers and toes. She and Spitfire had fallen, with her catapulting over his head. She woke up just before hitting the ground. Dawn cracked the black sky in the east before she fell asleep again.

When her alarm buzzed, Trish dragged herself out of bed. Instead of the usual butterflies, lead weights clanged together in her middle. They wouldn't have to insert weights in her saddle pad. She already had them.

Trish galloped the horses at the farm, but even the breeze couldn't blow away her worry.

"Let it go," her father said when she came back up to the house. "You can't let Spitfire know you're scared. Or the other horse that you'll ride first. No jockey in his right mind would be so foolish to attack again. Not with all the questions the racing commissioners have been asking. Just go out there and ride your best race ever."

Trish felt better after the pep talk. Her father was good at that. *And he's right. Nobody would be stupid enough to try something again.* She stuffed the nagging little doubt down—out of sight and mind. The purse was a good one today. And Runnin' On Farm needed a good purse.

Trish rode high in her stirrups, controlling the dancing Spitfire while scanning the other jockeys. She'd been in the winner's circle once already. Twice would be better than nice. Spitfire snorted and fought the bit.

Trish switched back to the monologue the colt was used to, and put the other entrants out of her mind . . . again. "Okay, fella, this is our chance. A long one today, and are you ever ready." Spitfire twitched his ears in cadence with her voice. He shied when a plastic bag flitted past and bonded to the fence. "Now behave yourself. Dad's got the glasses right on us."

On the canter back to the gates he shied again, this time at something only he could see. "Easy now, you're wasting your energy." Trish guided him into the number-five gate. "Now, we're going for the outside, you hear me?" As the horses settled for the gun, Trish crouched high on her mount's withers, ready for the thrust.

At the shot, Spitfire leaped through the opening. Instead of minding Trish's hands on the reins, he pulled toward the rail, aiming for an open space just to the left. Trish pulled him back, bringing his chin nearly to his chest, her arms straining with the effort. They were boxed in again. Horses in front and on both sides.

Both Trish and Spitfire saw the opening at the same moment. As Trish loosened the reins, the dreaded sound of a whip stung her ears. Spitfire screamed and leaped into the slight opening, knocking hard against the horse on the left.

Like dominos, two horses thrashed to the ground, one rider flying under their feet. Spitfire leaped over the balled-up jockey and landed hard on his right fore-leg. At his grunt of pain, Trish knew her horse was in trouble. But Spitfire refused her commands to slow. He leveled out, running free, chasing the three horses running in front.

While it seemed to Trish they'd been held back forever, they were only a furlong behind the leaders. Spitfire lengthened his stride, his belly low to the ground. Trish rode high over his withers, no longer fighting but assisting him all she could.

They drove past the third-place runner, then the second. At the mile post they caught the straining leader. Even with the saddle, neck and neck, each stride brought the black colt closer to victory.

The whip did the other horse no good. Spitfire ran him right into the ground to win by half a length. When Trish pulled him down to a trot, he began to limp. His heaving sides told her the effort he'd put forth to take the race. By the time they got to the winner's circle, Spitfire could harldy touch his right front hoof to the ground. Trish slid off him and ran her hand down his leg. The swelling popped up as she stroked.

"Dad, they did it again!"

CHAPTER 14

"Did you see anything? Could you tell who did it?"

Hal shook his head. "I must have moved the glasses off you just that second. The next thing I knew both horses were going down. It happened so quickly."

Trish smiled for the photographer, then turned her attention back to Spitfire. "Easy, fella," she smoothed his forelock and rubbed behind his ear. Spitfire leaned his head against her, all the while keeping his weight off the injured leg.

Hal stood after his inspection of the injury. "I'm pretty sure it's not broken, but we'll get an X-ray to be on the safe side. Let's get him back to the barn. Trish, you have another mount, right?"

"Yeah, I'll come down to the stalls as soon as I'm done." She shook her head as Spitfire limped slowly away. *There goes the Futurity.*

Scenes flashed in her mind as she trotted over to the dressing room. *If only I'd pulled back harder. I should* not *have let us get caught in that box. A GOOD jockey keeps her mount out of trouble. What's the matter with me?* She jerked open the door. The familiar aroma of liniment-steam, shampoo, and perfume greeted her. Today *she* smelled of mud and horse.

145

Trish quickly changed to the black and white silks, snapped the helmet piece in place, and picked up her whip. The thought of using it on some well-deserving jockey brought a grim smile to her face. *If only they could find out who hates my performance so much they'd whip my horse.*

"You okay?" one of the women asked.

"Yeah. How's the jockey that fell?"

"Broken arm. He must've gotten kicked by one of the other horses."

Trish gritted her teeth. "I'm sorry to hear that." *Now a jockey's been injured, too. Does a jockey or a horse have to get killed before this stops?* She was sure she felt a coolness from the other jockeys. *Do they think I'm at fault?* The new thought brought a lump to her throat. She left for the scales.

"Now you be careful, hear?" Bob Diego gave her a leg up. "Something funny is going on out there."

Trish nodded. "You don't think I . . . um-mm . . . that is . . ."

"No. Once—maybe an accident. Three times?" He shook his head. "Just bring this old lady up from behind. She doesn't mind mud in her face and she likes to chase the leaders, wear 'em down." He patted his mare's shoulder.

Trish did exactly as she was told. She held the mare back so she was slow coming out of the gate. Reins tight, Trish let the field pull ahead. When the runners strung out along the fence, she let the mare have her head on the outside. Every stride brought them closer to the trailing horse, past him and working on the next. Trish grinned. *This old lady sure knows her stuff.* Trish felt like she was only along for the ride.

When they passed the second-place runner, the rider went for his whip. Trish closed out her instinctive flinch and shouted her own encouragement. The mare stretched out even more and caught the furiously lunging lead. The number-one animal dropped back, spent before the finish line. The mare crossed a length ahead.

"Thanks." She slid to the ground in the winner's circle and handed the reins to Diego's trainer.

"Thank you." Bob Diego smiled for the flash and turned to Trish. "You did a good job. She was due for a win."

Trish trotted across the infield to the stables. She met horses on their way to the next race. "Please God" kept time with her feet, but this time it was for her horse.

Hal and David already had the leg wrapped in medicated mud bandage strips. Spitfire rested the tip of a hoof on the ground, taking all his weight on the remaining three good legs. He nickered when he saw Trish.

"No, it's not broken," Hal said before she could ask. "Let's get him home so we can work with him." Hal leaned against the wall. "David, you get the truck, and Trish, you lead him out."

Hal rested his head on the back of the seat as David drove out the back gate. By the time they reached Highway 205, the weary man snored softly.

Now, alone with her thoughts, Trish's anger came rolling back, threatening to drown her. She clenched her fists and jaw. *How could anyone deliberately hurt someone else—man or horse?* When her mind played with what might have been, she shuddered. "I didn't file a complaint!" She kept her voice low so her father wouldn't wake up.

"Dad did," David whispered.

"Good."

As soon as they arrived home, Hal went straight to bed and slept through the evening. Trish and David took turns applying ice packs to Spitfire's leg.

"What'd Dad say about his chances for the Futurity?" Trish asked as they turned off the lights for the night.

"Said not to give up hope, but chances are slim."

"It's just so unfair, so . . . so . . ."

"Bet the jock with the broken arm is ticked, too."

"And Mom?"

"What do you think?"

Trish chewed on her bottom lip. She could imagine what her mother was thinking.

Marge gave her daughter a quick hug, I-told-you-so written in her expression.

———

The next morning Trish wanted to stay with Spitfire, but wisely dressed for church, and was ready on time.

God, you're supposed to be taking care of us. That's what Dad always says. When she simmered down a bit, her nagger whispered almost imperceptibly, *You weren't hurt, were you? It could have been a lot worse.*

Trish couldn't think of a good answer. And with so much on her mind, she didn't hear much of the service.

———————

With the extra study hall, Trish didn't have to bring books home, but it also gave her extra time to brood. *Who, and why? And why hasn't the racing commissioner reported it yet? What is going on?*

Rhonda, Brad, and Trish worried over the situation like dogs with a bone. They dug up every memory and fact they could, discussed every jockey, and then repeated the process again. Nothing. They just didn't have all the pieces to the puzzle.

Trish spent every evening with the horses—packing Spitfire's leg, and galloping the others. Every time she saw the colt flinch or limp, she wanted to grind the culprit who caused the injury into the dirt.

"Trish, you've got to let this thing go," Hal told her one evening. "It's not your place to solve this. And *you* aren't the one to mete out justice or punishment." He smiled at her troubled expression.

"How can you be so calm? Don't you want to . . . to . . ."

"Get even?"

Trish nodded.

Hal shook his head. "Then I'd be just as guilty as they are. No, Tee, it's not worth it. Just let it go. And do your best."

By Wednesday the swelling was gone, and on Thursday Spitfire's leg was cool to the touch. When they clipped him to the hot walker, he still favored the leg but he was walking straight. Within half an hour, the leg heated up again. It was back to the barn for packs.

Friday morning Trish found a new card on her desk. "Vengeance is mine, I will repay" (Hebrews 10:30). Her father had added a line of his own. "He's better at it than we are."

Trish smiled grimly. *Then why doesn't He get on it?*

Friday the leg stayed cool after an hour on the walker.

"I think we're okay." Hal carefully felt every muscle and tendon. "But not working at all this week, I don't know, Tee." He shook his head. "I just don't know."

"You think we should scratch him?"

"He seems sound, but racing could injure it again." He patted Spitfire's neck. "Well, old boy, I guess we'll make the decision in the morning."

Trish had been praying all week, but her prayers that night included a note of panic. She'd been so sure God would heal her horse in time.

Saturday morning Spitfire trotted around the hot walker, snorting and playing with the ring and lead shank. Hal rubbed his chin once. "Let's do it." He turned and headed up to the house for breakfast. Trish danced beside him, much like Spitfire, in her exuberance. At one point she jogged backwards, arms raised in a victory clench.

"So you're going to do it." Marge shook her head, a frown creasing her forehead.

Trish knew her mother had been hoping they would give up the idea. But if they won the Portland Futurity . . . the next step would be the Santa Anita in California. And after that, the first Saturday in May.

Trish won on both mounts that afternoon. And while she watched carefully, no one bothered her. No whips, no screams of pain. No falling horses or jockeys. On the ride home, she voiced something that had been lurking at the back of her mind. "The attacks come only when I'm riding *our* horses."

"Naw," David disagreed. "The first time you were up on Anderson's gelding."

"I know. But he's from our stables. Maybe the dummy didn't know any differently."

"You may have something there," Hal agreed that evening when they were doing their post-race hash-over.

Trish went to bed with a solid weight in her middle. Tomorrow she would be back up on Spitfire—their own horse. She tried to swallow with a parched throat. *What if* . . . she shut her eyes tight against the "what if's" and tried to picture Jesus hugging the children. *I bet He loved horses, too!*

———————

It was Sunday morning. "Clearing by noon," David's clock radio announced as Trish padded down the hall to the shower. *That's one good thing*, she mused. It had been dry for three days. At least the track wouldn't be muddy. She let the hot water beat on her tight shoulders. Even her butterflies felt dormant. No aerial flips today, just heavy weights.

Halfway through the church service, the pastor announced that Hal Evanston would like to share a few words. Trish scrunched her legs against the pew so he could get by. At the same moment, she shot him a questioning look. What was going on?

Her father scanned the members of the congregation, smiled at his family. "I want to publicly thank all of you for your continuing support and prayers. I'm here today because our loving Father listens and cares for His children. The doctors were sure I would go fast, but they shot all their weapons at the cancer anyway. You, we all, prayed. That's an unbeatable combination—and Friday, the X-rays showed the proof. The tumors are receding."

The congregation broke out in spontaneous applause.

Hal waited. "We always know God is at work in us and for us even when we can't see what He is doing. This time He's allowed us to see the results. Again, thank you for your faithfulness to me and my family, and thank you, Father, for the gift of life." He bowed his head. "Amen."

Marge gripped Trish's hand. "He wanted to surprise you," she whispered.

Trish let the tears roll down her cheeks. They caught in the corners of her smile.

There wasn't a dry eye to be seen after the service. By the time everyone had hugged her father and mother, Trish felt full, to the point of spilling over.

Rhonda danced in place. She grabbed Trish's hands, then dropped them to hug her. "I am *so* happy."

"Me too." The words didn't begin to say what Trish was feeling. No words could.

The glow stayed with her all the way to the track.

Spitfire was in good spirits. When David lifted the colt's front hoof, Spitfire nudged him and sent him sprawling in the straw.

"Knock it off!" David picked up the hoof again.

Brad rubbed down the colt's opposite shoulder with a soft cloth. Spitfire reached around, nipped off Brad's crimson and gold baseball hat and tossed it in the corner.

Trish caught the giggles. She doubled over laughing at the looks on the guys' faces. Then Spitfire gave her a shove that toppled her on her rear in the straw.

This time David and Brad joined in the laughter. Spitfire pricked his ears and blew, reaching down to shower Trish with his warm, misty breath.

When Trish was back on her feet, the horse nudged against her chest, then rubbed one eye against her shoulder. She rubbed all his favorite places, all the while telling him how wonderful he was. He nodded in contentment.

"That horse is almost human." Rhonda leaned on the stall door. "Sorry I'm late, but it looks like you managed without me."

"You missed the clown act." Trish let herself out of the stall. "Come on, I've got another race before the Futurity. See you guys at the paddock." She picked up her bag in the tack room.

By the time she'd changed after the first race, Trish's butterflies were frisking full force. Until she saw her father in the saddling paddock.

"Just let God handle the race," he said as he boosted her up.

"Reading my mind again?"

"No, your face." He patted her knee. "And I know how you think and feel. Just go out there and do your best. That's all you can do. Let God take care of the rest."

Trish leaned forward to give Spitfire a big hug. She smoothed his mane to one side and gathered up her reins.

She tried to keep the black to a flat walk to conserve his energy, but Spitfire would have none of it. He jigged sideways, pulling against the lead rope in Brad's hands and against the reins.

"He sure is ready," Brad said from his perch on Dan'l's back.

"I hope so," Trish answered. "But he's never raced this far before." *And he's been penned up all week.*

A slow canter brought them to the gates. Trish took a deep breath and released it along with her plea, "Please God." The two words said it all.

Spitfire broke clean at the shot and drove straight down the middle of the track. He ran easily, as if nothing had happened. His twitching ears kept track of Trish's song, sung from high on his withers, and the horses around him. The field spread out going into the first stretch and when Spitfire eased over to the rail, Trish let him. By the three-quarters mark, Spitfire was running stride for stride with another horse. A sorrel and a gray ran two lengths in front, also side by side.

At the mile post, their running mate fell back and Spitfire gained on the two ahead, now running head to tail. Stride by stride the colt eased past the second place and gained on the front runner. The leading jockey went to his whip.

Trish could feel Spitfire waver. His breath came in thundering gasps. "Come on, fella," she shouted. "This is it. We're almost there. Come on."

Spitfire reached out one more time and hurtled over the finish line.

"And the winner by a nose is—Number three, Spitfire. Owner, Hal Evanston, and ridden by Tricia Evanston."

"You did it. You did it!" Trish pulled Spitfire down to a canter. Lather covered his shoulders and flew back when he shook his head. He slowed to a walk, still gasping for air. His sides heaved. Trish patted his neck, comforting him. As his breathing slowed, his head came up again. By the time they entered the winner's circle, he pricked his ears and rubbed his itchy forehead against Hal's arm.

Trish slid to the ground. Her knees wobbled so bad she hardly had the energy to unbuckle her saddle girth. David grinned at her. Hal hugged her and they all posed for the pictures. Trish plucked a rose from the wreath and handed it to her mother.

"Save this one for me, will you?"

Marge nodded, relief evident in the smile that fought the tears for first place.

Santa Anita, here we come, Trish thought as she stepped off the scales. *And after that . . .*

That evening David turned to the sports section of the local paper. The headline read, "Jockey on Probation." He read the article aloud. "Investigation has revealed that Emanuel Ortega, 19-year-old jockey at Portland Meadows, is the alleged attacker on Tricia Evanston and her mount on three occasions during the last several weeks." David rattled the paper. "All right!"

The article continued with a quote. "People like her

keep the rest of us from riding," Ortega said. "She's from a rich family and since she's the daughter of a owner, she gets the breaks we don't."

"Rich!" Tricia burst out. She stared at her father. "Rich!"

Hal shook his head. His laugh started down deep in his chest. David joined in, then Marge.

"But we are, you know." Hal tousled Trish's hair as she sat at his feet. "We're rich beyond measure."

ACKNOWLEDGMENTS

My thanks to Adele Olson, Prairie High Counselor and friend to students and their parents. Also to Tex Irwin, trainer at Portland Meadows, who so willingly shared his expertise. And thanks to Ruby MacDonald: reader, critiquer, and blessed friend.